P B 9

C000291588

IN PLAIN SIGHT

ADAM CROFT

BLACK CANNON
PUBLISHING

First published in Great Britain in 2019.

This edition published in 2021 by Black Cannon Publishing.

ISBN: 978-1-912599-66-0

A CIP catalogue record for this book is available from the British Library.

Printed and bound in Great Britain by Clays Ltd, Elcograf S.p.A.

MORE BOOKS BY ADAM CROFT

RUTLAND CRIME SERIES

KNIGHT & CULVERHOUSE CRIME THRILLERS

PSYCHOLOGICAL THRILLERS

- Only The Truth
- In Her Image
- Tell Me I'm Wrong
- The Perfect Lie
- Closer To You

KEMPSTON HARDWICK MYSTERIES

1. Exit Stage Left
2. The Westerlea House Mystery
3. Death Under the Sun
4. The Thirteenth Room
5. The Wrong Man

All titles are available to order from all good book shops.

Signed and personalised books available at adamcroft.net/shop

EBOOK-ONLY SHORT STORIES

- Gone
- The Harder They Fall
- Love You To Death
- The Defender

To find out more, visit adamcroft.net

Trinity Lloyd wasn't a fan of the late shift. Petrol stations were empty, soulless places at the best of times but it was even worse when she just wanted to get home to bed.

It wasn't made any easier by the fact that she had to get up at the crack of dawn the next morning for a nine o'clock lesson at Mildenheath College. Still, there were only four months left until she'd be a fully qualified childcare specialist.

Those thoughts were far from her mind, though, as she shuffled the display of Cadbury's Chocolate Buttons on the edge of the counter, trying to make them look somehow more appealing. She was constantly amazed at how many people impulse-bought them at the advertised 'incredible discount' despite the fact they were still almost twice the price of the convenience store down the road.

The owner claimed this was perfectly reasonable as

they were an 'out of town' petrol station, even though they were barely a couple of hundred yards outside the edge of Mildenheath — and still claimed Mildenheath as part of their address.

This was typical of Ian Gumbert, though, who the staff jokingly referred to as Call Me Mister, after his keenness that employees should refer to him respectfully as Mr Gumbert rather than simply Ian. His penchant for penny-pinching was notorious amongst the staff, and it was common knowledge that Gumbert didn't mind his businesses barely breaking even — the land they sat on was going to earn him a very nice retirement indeed when he finally decided to sell up.

For Trinity and the rest of the staff, it was just a job. They were left with almost complete autonomy, apart from the times when Gumbert would appear and ask for completely pointless changes to be made. Once, he insisted that *Heat* magazine should be on the left of *Hello!* and not — as it had been —the other way round, as it made the display look more 'balanced'. They'd smiled and nodded, acquiescing to his request, only to swap them back round again after he'd left.

Still, it was money in the back pocket for relatively easy, uninteresting and eventless work. Gumbert's sky-high prices meant locals very rarely filled up at his petrol stations, and it was only the occasional fill-up from an out-of-towner visiting Mildenheath and panicking on leaving the town's boundaries that kept them going.

Trinity had bigger ambitions in life. Her grandmother had died when she was just six years old, and it was only then that she realised Charissa had personally revolutionised childcare in Jamaica with her own small empire of nurseries. Ever since then, Trinity had wanted to follow in her footsteps. Of course, the childcare system in the UK was already well established, but the idea of working with children had stuck with Trinity ever since.

Her mother had wanted her to be a doctor. Either that or a lawyer. 'There's no money in childcare,' she used to say. 'Tell that to Grandma's forty-acre estate in Montego Bay,' Trinity would reply. She knew her mother was secretly pretty proud of her career choice. Deep down.

She might have been a little less happy with her daughter's present employment, though, if she'd seen the dark BMW estate pull up on the forecourt.

As the car came to a stop near the door, two men got out — one from the passenger seat, one from the back — and walked quickly and calmly into the shop, their faces obscured by balaclavas.

Before Trinity had even had a chance to register what was happening, she was greeted by the sight of a gun being pointed at her face. She didn't know one gun from another, but this one was longer than a pistol.

'The money. All of it. Now,' one of the men said, although she couldn't be sure which one it was. Everything was a bit of a blur. 'The bucket, under the counter,' another voice said.

She did as she was told, and bent down to retrieve the large rectangular bucket from under the counter, trying to remember how many staff members had told Gumbert it was a fucking stupid idea in the first place. All her brain could do to make light of the situation was to give her the thought that maybe this would convince him to step up his security measures in future. She knew that wouldn't happen, though.

As soon as she lifted the bucket above the level of the desk, the two men leaned over and snatched it, turning on their heels and leaving the shop almost as quickly as they'd entered it.

By the time they got back outside, the boot had been popped, ready for them to throw the bucket inside, slam the boot, get in the car and make good their escape.

Back inside the forecourt shop, Trinity's mind finally started to come to terms with what had happened, as she dropped to her knees and began to cry.

PC Theo Curwood brought the Volvo to just below sixty miles an hour before slowing to turn into the petrol station. Although the call hadn't been given the highest level of priority, Theo was less than a mile from the scene when it had come in, and was otherwise having a pretty quiet night. He knew it was possible to peak at well over seventy on that stretch of road, but there was no immediate threat to life — and he didn't fancy being responsible for one.

As he was pulling in, another call came across the radio announcing another robbery that had just occurred at a petrol station on Chancel Street.

Theo raised his eyebrows briefly, but wasn't particularly shocked. It was often the case that robberies would follow in quick succession as a gang tried to get as many results as they could before going back underground for a while until things calmed down. It wasn't unusual for a group of lads to come from out of town, hold up a few shops and disappear again within a few hours, before getting rid of their car and trying somewhere else a few weeks later.

The call asked for nearby units to attend the second robbery, which Theo knew would reduce the chances of a colleague attending this job with him. Late night single-crewing was becoming disappointingly frequent, and it was only a matter of time before an officer lost their life attending the wrong call on their own.

To the management bods, the fact that someone had been in this petrol station only minutes earlier wielding a firearm was irrelevant. To them, the immediate threat had now passed and there was no risk to life. Not at this partic-ular petrol station, anyway.

He got out of the car and made his way into the shop, careful to avoid leaving his own fingerprints on the door. If he was honest, he didn't see the point. There were probably hundreds of sets of prints all over the building, and he was pretty certain none of them belonged to the robbers.

He walked up to the counter and looked over the top of it, spotting a girl sitting with her knees tucked up to her chest, shaking and swaying from side to side.

'You okay, love? Do you need medical assistance?'

She shook her head. 'No. No. I'm fine.'

'My name's Theo, I'm a police officer. Are you able to stand up for me?'

Slowly, she got to her feet and tried to compose herself. 'Trinity. Trinity Lloyd.'

'That your name?'

She nodded again.

'Okay, Trinity. Are you the person who phoned the police?'

Another nod.

'Right. Is there anywhere we can go to sit down and have a chat? Maybe lock the front door as well. We don't want any members of the public walking through a potential crime scene.'

Trinity did as she was told, walking over to the front doors and turning two latches, one at the top and one at the bottom, before leading Theo through into an office behind the counter area.

It seemed more like a dumping ground than a working office, the desk stacked high with papers, the top of a computer monitor just peering out above them.

'So. Can you tell me what these people looked like?' Theo asked.

'No. They were wearing balaclavas.'

'How many of them were there?'

'Two. Although, thinking about it, there must have been a third one in the car because one got in the back and the other one got in the passenger side.'

'Okay. And can you describe them for me?' Theo asked, taking down notes. Normally, he'd sit down with a witness and go methodically through everything they'd seen and experienced, but Trinity seemed to be quite happy to lead the way and offer up what she could, so he decided he'd jot down what he could and formalise it later.

'Not really, no. They were both dressed in black with black balaclavas.'

'When you say dressed in black, what items of clothing were they?'

Trinity seemed to think about this for a moment. 'Uh, one had like a black denim jacket and black trousers. The other one I think was a sort of jumper over black jeans. But I might be wrong about that. It all happened so quickly.'

Theo knew she almost certainly would be wrong — most witnesses were — and many felt they had to give as much information as possible, despite the fact their brains hadn't actually registered any of it. As a result, people tended to inadvertently add detail or description which never existed — something which tended to make the police's job a lot harder. Multiple witnesses were useful in finding common threads, but in a situation where only one person witnessed an event, it would be extremely difficult to put any weight on what they said unless it tallied with other evidence.

'And did they say anything?' he asked.

'Yeah. One of them told me to give him the money, and the other one was just trying to get me to go faster. I think. I don't really remember. I'm sorry.'

'That's okay, don't worry about it. Do you remember any of the words or phrases they definitely used? Did they call each other by name?'

Trinity shook her head slowly. 'No. I remember one of them said to get the bucket from underneath the counter. That was a bit weird as no-one knows about that except for staff.'

'The bucket?'

'Yeah. I know, it's stupid. In some petrol stations there's a hole in the counter. So when the till gets too full of notes, you roll them, put them in this little canister and drop them into the hole. Then they go down a chute into a secure area in the basement. Our boss decided we didn't need to spend the money on safes and security systems, so ours just goes through the hole and into a big trough sort of thing under the counter.'

'That sounds risky.'

'It's stupid. But that's what he's like. It was bound to happen at some point.'

Theo's mind was already racing. Although he probably wouldn't play any part in the ongoing investigation, he knew where he'd focus his priorities. To him, it sounded very much like an inside job. Someone knew the petrol station had lax security measures. Someone knew the cash canisters landed in a bucket under the counter. A disgruntled ex-employee, perhaps? They'd need to get a list of everyone who'd left the company in the past few years. He thought an insurance job was unlikely, especially as the insurance company would almost certainly reject their claim when they discovered how poor the owner's security measures were.

'Which one of them mentioned the bucket, do you remember?' he asked.

Trinity shook her head. 'No. They both spoke but I don't know which was which. One was standing behind the other one and their balaclavas went over their mouths.'

'And how tall were they?'

'I dunno. I don't even know how tall I am. They were both the same sort of height. Maybe the same as you? I don't know. Sorry.'

'That's alright. But not abnormally tall or short or anything?'

'Not that I noticed, no.'

'Any other distinguishing features?'

'I don't think so. Sorry.'

He was about to tell her it was alright and she didn't need to keep apologising when a call came in over his radio. Even though it was standard for officers to have an earpiece fitted, Theo found it uncomfortable and distracting and tended to have it clipped to his shoulder with the volume turned up, so he could hear if there was anything he needed to respond to without it getting in the way. It seemed Trinity's hearing was sharper than his, though.

'Catford Road? That's one of ours,' she said, commenting on the robbery that had just been phoned in and radioed out.

'How do you mean?' Theo asked.

'The petrol station. It's owned by the same person. He's

got three around Mildenheath. It can't be a coincidence that they've done two of his in the same night.'

Theo had to agree, but knew that there was a possibility it was actually even worse than that.

'When you say he's got three sites, which one is the third?' he asked, fearing the answer before she'd even said it.

'Chancel Street. Why?'

The media often liked to talk about crimewaves, but crime in Mildenheath almost always came in waves. The curious setup of the county's policing structure meant that Mildenheath CID's major incident team had a varied workload, which almost always centred on the town itself. Wider county matters and major crimes from outside the town were taken care of at county headquarters at Milton House.

It was an interesting quirk of both geography and local politics that Mildenheath had not only managed to retain its own satellite CID department but also control over handling major incidents occurring in and around the town.

There were plenty of people who sought to upset that particular apple cart and move all power to Milton House, but DCI Jack Culverhouse was certainly not one of them. As long as the structure remained intact until his retirement, he'd be happy.

One downside was that he was almost always listed as the on-call DCI. In his absence, his nemesis Malcolm Pope was usually listed as the on-call commander, and this was one of the reasons why Jack Culverhouse almost never took a day off. The possibility of accidentally handing over control of a major incident to Pope was enough to ensure he picked up all the hours he could and resisted all calls to take a step back.

It had, of course, had an impact both on his health and his personal relationships. It would be impossible for it not to have done. But, in a perverse way, throwing himself into his work had helped enormously and he was grateful to be able to do something truly rewarding.

In recent years, work had provided a welcome distraction from his personal life — ironic since it was his obsession with work which had caused most of his problems in the first place. Things were starting to look up, though. His daughter, Emily, was back living with him after her mother left the family home with her when she was only a few years old. Now when he looked at her, just a couple of months away from her sixteenth birthday, he was proud of the young woman Emily was becoming.

She'd proved to be a challenge, of course. No kid with her background and upbringing wouldn't. Her mother had battled her own personal demons for years and hadn't given two thoughts to burdening Emily with them at the same time.

Jack wondered how many of Helen's traits and issues

had passed on to Emily, having noticed cut marks — both old and fresh — on her arms. He'd tried to bring it up with her but had never quite known how. It was an awkward relationship at times. The years they'd had apart meant he found it difficult to raise these sorts of issues with her and often chose to keep the peace instead.

Each call provided him with a mixture of emotions, even after so many years in the job. There was anticipation, excitement and, of course, annoyance at the fact that the call would always come either in the middle of the night or the middle of the supermarket.

This time it wasn't quite either, but he had been hoping to hit the sack and get some sleep before heading in the next morning for his normal shift.

Unfortunately for him, the ringing of his mobile phone put paid to that idea. Glancing at the screen, he could see it was work.

'I hope it's not bad timing,' the caller said.

'Not at all. I was sitting by my front door with my shoes on waiting for you to call.'

The caller ignored Culverhouse's trademark sarcasm and continued. 'We've got multiple armed robberies at petrol stations in and around Mildenheath. Three at present, all under the Gumbert's brand name.'

'Right. Any others?'

'No. Not that we've had reports of.'

A few thoughts flashed through Culverhouse's mind: a grudge, an insurance scam, just plain bad luck.

'Put all independent petrol stations in the area on high alert, just in case they're targeting the small guys. Warn all the major chains, too. Who owns the Gumbert's chain?'

'A bloke by the name of Ian Gumbert.'

'Right. Get hold of him and arrange for someone to meet him for questioning. He's either being targeted specifically or he's responsible. Either way, we need to speak to him.'

4

Wendy Knight smiled as she watched Xav snoring open-mouthed beside her. Falling asleep in front of the TV was one of those quirks and foibles she loved about him, but which no-one in their right mind would list as facets of their ideal man. That certainly didn't stop her finding them incredibly endearing, though.

Xav hadn't officially moved in, but he was doing a pretty good impression of it. He'd recently decided to put his own house on the market and move in with Wendy, although he hadn't yet managed to find a buyer. Wendy thought that was a bit odd, especially as she'd had to push him to list the house in the first place, but she didn't see any point in questioning it just yet. At worst, he was just another commitment-phobic man.

She didn't hold it against him, though. He'd been incredibly supportive towards her and had urged her to take her inspector's exams — something she'd been considering but avoiding for some time. She'd given herself all the excuses under the sun, but when it came down to it she realised that deep down she felt uncomfortable at the prospect of matching – and potentially exceeding — the rank her own father had achieved before his untimely death.

She knew, too, that Xav had been hurt in the past and he'd need to take things at his own pace. Neither of them had come into this relationship without baggage, and as far as Wendy was concerned it was great just to have someone who she could connect with, without the worry that something was going to go horribly wrong. To many other women, Xavier Moreno might have come across as a bit of a wet blanket, but to Wendy he was safe. And safety was the most important thing in her life.

Balancing her private life and her career had proven difficult — as any police officer would easily attest — but Xav knew the score. He'd been part of civilian police staff for a few years, working in computer forensics, and had recently decided to take the next step on his own career ladder. He'd decided he wanted to become a police officer, specialising in the same field but giving him a direct police role with greater responsibility and the opportunity to get involved in spearheading the fight against cyber crime.

Wendy didn't pretend to know anything about computers or cyber crime, which is precisely why she'd had to call on Xav so often and the two had eventually become close.

It was the first time in many years she'd let someone else into her life. The last time that had happened, she'd fallen hard and fast and it had ended in tragedy. That was the sort of heartbreak she just couldn't go through again.

Before then, the only real man in her life had been her father, Detective Inspector Bill Knight. He'd been her hero when she was a child, and her family had been devastated by his early and untimely death.

Sometimes, she wondered whether her reticence in allowing Xav into her life had been because she somehow felt guilty at replacing her father as the man who always had her heart. With her last lover, Robert Ludford, she'd barely had time to sit back and think about such things, but since then she'd grown older and far more philosophical.

She looked again at Xav, his throat wobbling slightly as he snored. She knew if she woke him up now he'd claim he'd been watching TV all along and hadn't fallen asleep — not even for a second. She didn't know why he did it, but it made her laugh. It was just another harmless foible which amused her and endeared him to her.

Tomorrow was Saturday. Although she had to work, Xav was a little more fortunate in his working hours and tended to stick to a solid Monday to Friday, nine til five. There was overtime available, and he often took it if he knew Wendy would be working anyway, but tomorrow was a day off for him.

She leaned over, kissed him on the head and switched off the light. At some point, he'd wake up and make his way quietly upstairs, slipping into bed beside her. She wouldn't notice. But in the morning she'd wake up and he'd be there, asleep again, allowing her to kiss him on the head once more before she left for work.

That suited her perfectly. That suited her very well indeed.

5

In many ways, Jack was pleased about Mildenheath Police's staff shortages and swingeing budget cuts. For starters, it meant he was often able to get out of the office and speak to witnesses himself — something which would have been left to DCs or uniformed constables in most other situations.

Jack had read the notes written up by Theo Curwood, as well as Trinity Lloyd's statement detailing Ian Gumbert's relaxed attitude towards security. Jack wasn't the sort of man to suffer fools gladly and had been sorely tempted to summon Gumbert to Mildenheath Police Station to speak to him, but there was something to be said for seeing a person in their native environment.

People tended to be a lot more relaxed in their own homes or on neutral ground — something which almost never happened when they were sitting in a police inter-view room. He was always keen to 'type' people, too —

something which could easily be done by taking a good look at the person's home.

It wasn't necessarily true to say that people with nicer homes didn't commit crimes, but there were certainly some telltale signs in the form of pride in one's surroundings which could tell Jack a lot about a person.

Ian Gumbert's house was a little less impressive than he'd imagined for a man who owned three petrol stations. It was situated in the nice-enough village of Peal End, on a road of twenty or so detached houses and bungalows. It looked to Jack as if it had been built somewhere around the seventies, and he immediately formed an impression of a local businessman who was perhaps a few years past retirement age and who'd bought this house as a new-build some forty or so years earlier. It had the look of a house which had been loved, played home to a growing family but had since begun to look a little tired.

That description could just as easily have applied to its owner, who opened the front door and welcomed Jack inside with a voice that exuded warmth and a face that had given up twenty years earlier.

'You caught anyone yet?' Gumbert asked, as he walked through to the kitchen and started to make Jack a cup of tea he hadn't asked for.

'Not yet, no. We're working on it. We're going to need as much information as we can get to improve our chances, which is where you come in.'

'Well, I'll do my best. But I'm not quite sure what I

can do.'

'You'd be surprised,' Jack said, switching on his portable recorder. He wasn't one for taking down notes, nor did he relish the thought of writing up a long-hand statement for Gumbert to sign. 'First of all, can you run me through what you already know about what happened last night?'

Gumbert sighed and leant back against the kitchen counter, arms crossed over his chest. 'Probably a lot less than you. All my petrol stations got robbed at gunpoint.'

'And who called you to let you know?'

'Black girl from Whitecliff Road.'

'Would that be Trinity Lloyd?' Jack asked, having already read the notes from the scene and finding himself uncharacteristically shocked at someone else's casual references to race.

'That's the one. Although she's a half-cast. Not a proper black.'

'I think Afro-Carribean is the term,' he replied, feeling the icy glare of Wendy Knight in her absence. 'In her witness report it says the thieves stole buckets from under the counter. Staff members at the other two sites said the same thing. Can you tell me what those buckets were used for?'

Gumbert let out a small laugh which implied this was a rather silly and trivial matter that he'd explained satisfactorily on many occasions before. 'They're safety deposit boxes, not buckets. When the tills get too full, staff use them to deposit cash.'

'And how are those boxes secured?'

'They're under the counter. No-one knows they're there except for the staff.'

'Somebody clearly did know they were there. They went straight for them.'

'Thieving little shits.'

'Is it not more normal to have a locked deposit box located somewhere else, out of the reach of anyone on the shop floor?'

Gumbert leaned forward slightly, in an almost patronising manner. 'Listen here. I've been running petrol stations for over forty years. We're the only independent brand left in the county which hasn't been taken over by Shell, BP or one of the other big boys. I know what I'm doing.'

Jack resisted the temptation to suggest that there might be a reason why his petrol stations were the only ones Shell and BP didn't want to buy. 'Do you know how much money was in the buckets?' he asked.

'Safety deposit boxes. And no, I'd have to go back through the receipts and tally it up against what was left in the tills. But each site turns over just shy of fifteen thousand a week.'

'And how much of that would you estimate might have been in each bucket?'

'Safety deposit box.'

'How much?'

'All of it.'

Culverhouse looked at him for a moment. 'All of it?'

'It gets taken to the bank on a Saturday morning. That's usually what I'd be doing right about now,' he said, checking his watch. 'Doesn't seem much point this week.'

'So let me get this straight. At the end of every night your staff cash up the tills, dump the money in a bucket — safety deposit box — and leave it there on the shop floor until Saturday morning?'

'It's not quite as ridiculous as you make out, but that's the gist of it, yes.'

'When presumably you come along, pop it in the back of your Renault Espace and queue up at Barclays with it?'

'I'm afraid I don't much like your tone, Detective Chief Inspector. Like I said, I've been running petrol stations for forty years and we've never had an incident like this in our history.'

'And I've been investigating robberies for almost as long and I can completely agree with you. What about panic switches? CCTV?'

Gumbert sat down and sighed heavily. 'I'm old school, you see. I grew up in Mildenheath. No-one ever used to lock their doors. Kids played freely in the streets. We didn't have to worry about armed robbers.'

'Of course you didn't. You were a kid. You didn't even know what an armed robber was.'

'We didn't need to. The world was a safer place. There was a sense of community spirit.'

Jack decided against trying to point out that crime had actually fallen heavily since Gumbert was a kid, but he thought it futile arguing against a man whose arsenal contained only doe-eyed childhood memories.

'So no panic switches? No CCTV?'

'I've got dummy cameras installed on all my forecourts and inside the shops,' Gumbert replied.

'Dummy cameras?'

Jack was starting to get a good measure of the type of person Ian Gumbert was. There was just no telling the man that he'd been foolish and naive. He did things his way and that was that. Any unfortunate consequences arising from that were not his fault.

'I think you'll find it's been proven that CCTV is most valuable as a deterrent,' Gumbert said.

'That theory's not holding much water right now, is it? An armed gang have just brazenly walked into every single branch of your business and cleared out the entire week's earnings.'

Jack watched closely for Gumbert's response. The man didn't seem to show any signs of distress or remorse at what had happened. There was definite anger at the people who'd done this, but it was tempered by a huge amount of calm and sangfroid.

'Oh, exactly,' Gumbert said. 'It was a brazen act. They'll have left evidence all over the place, I'm sure of it. It won't take you long to catch them.'

Jack had been half hoping he'd say something like that.

'I'm afraid it's not quite that straightforward. This sounds like an organised gang. They knew where they were targeting and why. We've not had any reports of any other robberies from any locations other than your three fore-courts. That means you were most likely targeted specifi-cally. These sorts of gangs know exactly what they're doing. They're very aware of forensics and only make a hit when they're certain they're going to get away with it. If there'd been some extra information to help us — CCTV evidence, say — then our chances would be better. But as things stand I've got to be realistic with you and tell you the chances of catching these people are extremely slim.'

Ian Gumbert looked as if he'd been shot in the head with a crossbow bolt. It was clear to Jack that he'd genuinely believed the police could just turn up, take a sole witness account from a young girl who'd just had a gun pointed in her face and solve the crime with a bit of detec-tive's intuition. The man was clearly deluded.

'It's clearly a targeted attack, Mr Gumbert. Can you think of anyone who might have wanted to do this to you? Anyone at all?'

Gumbert sat for a moment, staring into space, then slowly shook his head.

'No. No. No-one.'

'Any business disagreements recently? Disgruntled ex-employees? Fallings out in your personal life?'

Jack knew where he had his money. Whoever had organised this not only knew that security at the three fore-courts was lax, but also that the entire week's takings were kept in an unsealed box below the counter. He didn't suppose it was any coincidence, either, that the robberies took place just hours before the takings were to be banked — maximising their haul. This had clearly been a very cleverly planned job, designed for maximum impact.

Gumbert shook his head again. 'No. No, I can't think of anybody.'

'Take some time over it. You don't even need to tell us today. Keep my number close at hand and call if you think of anybody, okay? Personally, I'd be thinking along the lines of employees or ex-employees. Whoever did this had a huge amount of information on the way your businesses are run. The chances of them having guessed everything are slim to none. If you haven't got an ex-employee with a grudge, you've got a mole.'

Gumbert slowly turned his head to make eye contact with Jack.

'You mean someone working for me tipped them off?'

Jack shrugged. 'Like I say. It's entirely possible. We'll need a full list of all your current employees and people who've worked for you in, say, the past two years. We'll start there. Run a few background checks, see if there's anyone that jumps out.'

Although Jack didn't think Gumbert's face could drop any more, he was wrong. The man turned white almost instantly.

'What is it, Mr Gumbert?'

Gumbert swallowed hard. 'There is somebody.'

6

DCI Jack Culverhouse's briefings were legendary amongst those at Mildenheath CID. There was no predicting how they'd go or which format they'd take. It all depended on his mood.

The level of autonomy Culverhouse and his team were given was something they didn't take for granted, but certainly made the most of.

The atmosphere was generally far more relaxed than in most major incident teams, although the pressure tended to be far greater. The whole team was acutely aware that they were only in existence because of their success rate. One slip-up — one failed case — and it'd give the force's superiors the perfect reason to close down Mildenheath CID and subsume everything into county headquarters at Milton House.

It was almost completely unheard of for the same team

to stick together from case to case, but Mildenheath's core major incident team had remained almost untouched for a number of years.

There was no conventional organisation chart, but Detective Sergeant Wendy Knight was almost universally considered to be Culverhouse's right-hand woman. This was largely due to the fact that she was the only member of the team with enough ambition to step up to the plate.

The ageing Detective Sergeant Frank Vine was eyeing retirement rather than a promotion, and DS Steve Wing had found his comfort point at Sergeant: enough money to live on, and enough responsibility to live without.

Detective Constable Debbie Weston had never had a desire to become a sergeant, despite being told many times over the years that she should. She was happy seeing out her work years doing the menial tasks, flying under the radar and often providing the technical breakthrough which led to the identification of a killer. She had, though, been taking a leave of extended absence to look after her mother, who was on her last — apparently very long — legs down on the south coast.

The team's newest recruit, DC Ryan Mackenzie, had thrown Culverhouse into something of a tailspin. Although the DCI had expected the anonymous new recruit to be a young man he could mold into a protégé of his very own, he'd been a little disappointed to discover Ryan Mackenzie was a young lesbian and vegan with strong ideas and morals — many of which were opposed to his own.

The desire for a protégé had been strong in Culver-house. He'd taken that role himself on joining Mildenheath CID all those years ago, working under the legendary Jack Taylor. The closest he'd come to forming an officer in his own mould was a young officer called Luke Baxter, who had been tragically taken from them in a showdown with the Mildenheath Ripper four years earlier.

Jack Culverhouse knew he didn't have many years left in his role. He'd either get fed up and chuck in the towel, be shuffled into a back office or pensioned off in a 'reorganisation scheme' or drop dead at his desk one day. His blood pressure had been through the roof for years, and the job had taken a heavy toll on his private life.

Retirement was never really going to be an option for him, though. The force was too severely understaffed for them to get rid of him voluntarily, and if fossils like Frank Vine were able to carry on working with one foot in the grave he was sure he still had a few years left in him yet.

'I presume you've all read the documentation on the three armed robberies in and around Mildenheath last night,' he said, knowing full well that one or two of them wouldn't have. Despite — or perhaps because of — this, he moved swiftly on. 'So, a quick update on where everyone is and which jobs have been assigned to everyone. Ryan's going through the list of current and ex-employees, cross-referencing that with the PNC to see if any of them have form. Steve and Frank are going through CCTV from the surrounding area to see if we can track the movements of the BMW before and after the incidents. I'll be overseeing the investigation as your Emperor and Overlord, as well as speaking to anyone of interest. Detective Sergeant Knight will be accompanying me on those trips and in the meantime will make me copious amounts of black coffee. Any questions on any of that?'

'Yeah, one lump or two?' Steve Wing joked.

'If you're talking about you and Frank, two. Now, we've already got statements from Trinity Lloyd, the girl who was on duty at the Whitecliff Road forecourt and Ian Gumbert, who owns all three branches. Statements from both of them show that security on the forecourts was lax, to say the least. Gumbert seemed not to give a shit until I pointed out that we couldn't just click our fingers and put the perpetrators in jail. Now he's experiencing what a more eloquent person might call a brown trouser moment. The only cameras on his forecourts are dummies. There are no panic alarms. The week's takings were kept in a box under the counter. All in all, it's an absolute fucking shitshow but unfortunately we're contractually obliged to try and do our best for him. As luck would have it, he poked and prodded his deluded little brain and came up with something which might help us.'

He gestured towards Wendy, who stood up and pointed to the image of a young man, which was pinned to the board behind Jack.

'This is Damian King. He spent time at Her Majesty's pleasure after being found guilty of a double assault when he kicked the living daylights out of two guys in a local nightclub. Apparently, he was convinced they were both leering over his girlfriend. Turns out not only was he wrong, he was very wrong. The two men were a gay couple enjoying a night out together and were definitely not interested in King's girlfriend in any way, shape or form. Regardless, one of the men had to have a steel plate inserted into his jaw and the other has had occasional epileptic seizures since the incident.'

'Nice bloke,' Ryan said.

'Nice enough for Ian Gumbert to give him the opportunity to get back on his feet with a job at one of his petrol stations, anyway,' Wendy replied.

Jack snorted. 'According to Gumbert, he's no Good Samaritan — as if we didn't already know that. Apparently Damian King is the son of an old family friend, Marsha King. Marsha leant on Gumbert and asked him to take a chance on her boy because he'd made a huge mistake and was dreadfully sorry. As if we haven't heard that one before.'

Wendy jumped in to continue the story. 'Unfortunately, Damian King wasn't the reformed character his mum made him out to be. Gumbert caught him with his hand in the till. Almost literally. He'd suspected him of being on the take, so came in before his shift one day and wrote *Damian is a tea leaf* on all the notes with an ultraviolet pen. He came back at the end of the shift and asked him to empty out his pockets. He had eighty quid in marked notes. He claimed he'd exchanged them for some smaller notes, but on closer inspection Gumbert found the takings in the till were down. Funnily enough, by almost exactly eighty quid.'

'How did he think he was gonna get away with that?' Steve piped up. 'I mean, most shops will expect their takings to be off by a few quid because of mistakes and stuff, but eighty quid?'

'I think the problem is he *didn't* think,' Wendy replied. 'He had his eye on the goal and didn't think it through, clearly. Same as he didn't think it through before kicking those guys' heads in.'

'Let's not forget he's shown himself to be a retaliator, too. Look what he did to those gay blokes,' Culverhouse said, eliciting a wince from a couple of members of the team. 'If he thinks someone's wronged him in some way, he reacts. Badly. Now, we need to bear in mind he's not gone out and done these robberies himself on his pushbike. This was an organised gang. They knew what they were doing. They were armed. We need to probe links, see who King's in contact with. He's shit at covering his tracks, so it wouldn't surprise me if there were text messages or some sort of evidence of communication we could find. If it's him, it'll be there.'

'Reasonable grounds for arrest?' Steve piped up.

'Not yet. We need something more. But I'll go round and see if he's up for a voluntary interview. See what we can get. DS Knight, you're coming with me.'

7

Jack and Wendy knew from his pictures on the Police National Computer that Damian King was a distinctive-looking guy. He was tall, stooped slightly from the shoulders and had a hooked nose that reminded them of a plague doctor from medieval times.

At first glance, he didn't look like the sort of man who'd be able to swing a punch, never mind put two people in hospital. They knew he had, though, so there was no telling what else he was capable of.

He still lived at home, although not in one of the roughest areas of town. It turned out that Damian King wasn't another product of the failed system or the never-ending cycle of poverty, crime and disillusionment, but had actually come from a pretty normal family in a pretty normal area of Mildenheath.

They recognised him as soon as he opened the door.

'Damian King? Detective Chief Inspector Jack Culver-house. This is Detective Sergeant Wendy Knight. Can we come in?'

The usual practice would be to have let King know he had nothing to worry about. There were numerous stories within the police service about officers who'd had someone open the door to them and immediately faint or freak out, thinking they were there to tell them one of their loved ones had been found dead. But, as far as Jack was concerned, he was in no mood to make Damian King feel at ease.

'Why, what's it about?' King asked.

'We'd rather talk inside if that's alright with you.'

'Are you arresting me?'

'No, we just want to talk to you.'

'Well you can piss off then. I ain't talking to you.' With that, King went to push the door shut. Jack put his foot in the way.

'I'm more than happy to arrest you if you like. I can authorise a full search of your house and your body. If you're extra lucky, I'll even ask them to wear gloves. Or you can just let us in and offer us a cup of tea. Entirely up to you.'

King looked at them for a moment, surveying them as if they were travelling salesmen, then stood back and watched them walk into his house.

'Mum not in?' Jack asked.

'She's at work. And I know you ain't got shit, so don't go threatening me again, alright?'

'I don't do threats, Damian. I do promises.'

'Bullshit. If you think you've got enough to search my house, you've got enough to arrest me. But you didn't, innit. Cos you've got nothing.'

'Nothing on what?' Jack asked.

'You tell me.'

'Alright. Get that kettle on and I will.'

King did as he was told.

'So,' Jack said, sitting at the kitchen table. 'How's work?'

'Not doing much at the moment. Had a few bits going on.'

'You were working at the petrol station weren't you?' he asked, watching King's eyes carefully.

'I was. For a bit.' His body language and demeanour gave nothing away, but that didn't surprise Jack. Some people managed to train themselves to not incriminate themselves. He doubted King was one of those, though he didn't seem entirely surprised to discover that they'd done their research on him.

'What happened?'

'I left.'

'Yeah, I got that. Were you sacked or did you resign?'

'I was asked to resign. So both. Neither. Whatever.'

'What for?'

King sighed. 'You know what for. Why do you lot always have to do this stupid dance where you ask me things you already know the answer to?'

'Because that's how it works. We need to hear your side of things.'

'I don't lie. And anyway, that fat prick said he weren't gonna tell the police.'

'Which fat prick is this?' Wendy asked, as if the words weren't even an insult.

'Ian. The bloke who owns the petrol station. He told me he wouldn't get the police involved, 'cos of my record and that.'

Jack looked at Wendy for a moment before speaking to King. 'This isn't about you nicking money from the till, Damian. At least not that particular incident, anyway. Where were you last night?'

'Here. At home.'

'All night?'

'From about half seven, yeah. I've got this bloody tag on, ain't I?' he said, lifting the leg of his jogging bottoms to reveal an ankle tag. 'Can't go anywhere between nine at night and six in the morning.' That was something that hadn't been apparent from their brief background checks into King, but which could provide valuable evidence.

'So that thing will show us you were at home all night last night?'

'It'll show you everywhere I've been, innit. It tracks everything.'

Except phone calls and encrypted text messages, Wendy thought, sure that any plans to organise an armed robbery would've been done much more secretly than King rocking up at his associates' houses.

Jack waited until he had a good view of King's face before landing the next question out of nowhere.

'Did you know all three of Ian Gumbert's petrol stations were robbed last night?'

'No,' King replied, without showing much emotion.

'Five blokes rocked up in a BMW with shotguns, which they pointed in the faces of the cashiers. One of them was a young college girl.' Jack had deliberately mentioned five robbers rather than three, to see if King questioned or corrected this later. If he did, he'd know he was lying.

'Jesus. She alright?'

'Physically. She'll be offered support.'

'Well I don't know what you want me to do, but I hope you catch them.'

'Do you?' Jack asked.

King locked eyes with him. 'Yeah. It's not right doing that to people.'

'Even to people like Ian Gumbert? A man you swore revenge against?'

King's face dropped slowly, before breaking into a smile as he nodded his head slowly. 'Alright. I see what this is all about. You reckon I did it, don't you? Asking about the petrol station, about my tag, trying to shit me up by saying about the girl what got a gun in her face. Alright. Yeah, alright. I'm saying nothing until you arrest me and get me a solicitor. Til then, you can fuck off, alright?'

'Shall I write that word for word in my notes?'

'Write what you like, cunt.'

'I probably won't write that, if I'm honest. Plays havoc with the spellcheck.'

Wendy interjected. 'It really would be better if you spoke to us and answered our questions, Damian. We're not here to try and catch you out. We just want to try to find the people responsible. The people who pointed a gun in that young girl's face.'

'Can't blame me for that,' King said.

'We're not trying to. Look at it from our point of view. We've got to follow any leads we have and speak to anyone who might possibly crop up as a person of interest. And, you've got to be honest with yourself, you're going to be one of them.'

'What, because I used to work there?' By now, King was starting to become visibly angry. Culverhouse jumped on the opportunity.

'No, because you've got previous for kicking two blokes' heads in and got the sack from the same petrol station for nicking money out the till. Now, you might be completely innocent and yes, maybe you were sitting at home watching Four Weddings and a Funeral, but it doesn't look great, does it?'

King looked at him for a moment. 'Nah. You're right. I don't like Hugh Grant either.'

Jack had to admit to himself that he got a little thrill when someone played him back at his own style. He liked the chase, the battle of wits and the banter he was able to get going with somebody — just before slapping a pair of cuffs on them and chucking them in a cell. But he knew that wasn't going to be an option with Damian King. Not today, anyway.

'Would you really rather we did this with search warrants, Damian?' Jack asked.

King looked at him and smiled.

'Bring it on.'

8

Jack Culverhouse slammed his car door a little harder than usual, before letting out a large sigh.

'Well I thought that went alright,' Wendy said, knowing exactly which buttons to push to wind her colleague up.

'Fuck off,' Culverhouse said quietly.

'If it's him, something'll crop up. Like you said, he's showed he's pretty hopeless when it comes to thinking ahead and covering his tracks.'

'It's the time factor, though. If he's involved he knows we'll be back, and now he's got the chance to start hiding stuff. We've given him a head start.'

It wasn't often Wendy felt sorry for Jack, but she was starting to feel his pain and frustration.

'He might not be involved in any way. In which case it's a good job we didn't arrest him. And if he is involved, we'll find something.'

Culverhouse shook his head. 'I've been doing this job long enough to know when someone's hiding something. And that shit with the ankle tag? It's bollocks. Do you know how easy those things are to get off? It's a joke. They're practically voluntary.'

'I think they're better now than they used to be. If he'd been out robbing petrol stations last night, we'd know about it.'

'He doesn't need to have even left the house. That's the beautiful thing. Do I think he was in the car or carrying the gun? Not a chance. He'll have set someone up to do the legwork. My money says he met someone while he was in prison and he's kept in touch, tipped them off and offered them a big share of the takings in exchange. I mean, come on — maybe he even told them they could keep the lot. His kick comes from doing Gumbert over. Surely even Damian King's not stupid enough to walk around with thousands of pounds in stolen notes in his pocket.'

'I don't see why not,' Wendy said. 'He's already done just that with eighty quid. And let's be fair — that's a pretty ambitious take from a till. Difficult to explain that away. I can't imagine him not wanting a piece of forty-five grand.'

Culverhouse chuckled slightly. 'See. I knew you thought he was involved.'

'No, I'm just saying that if he is I don't think the ankle tag can really be used as evidence. We'll need to do cell site analysis on his mobile. See if that left his house last night, or if it's gone walkabout without his ankle tag at any point. It's easy enough to go out and forget your mobile, but it's a bit more difficult to accidentally leave your ankle at home.'

'You've not met some of the officers I've worked with over the years, then,' Culverhouse muttered, starting his engine and pulling out into the road. 'Either way. There's something not quite right about him.'

'To be fair, you say that about everybody.'

'And I'm usually right. You get to spot the signs. Something's definitely going on. He's as shady as anything. And he makes shit tea.'

9

After having arrived back at Mildenheath Police Station, Jack was disappointed to see Chief Constable Charles Hawes walking towards him in the corridor.

It wasn't that he was disappointed to see the Chief Constable himself; more that he could read Hawes's face like a child's picture book and knew when it was going to be bad news.

It wasn't unusual to see Hawes at Mildenheath, either. Even though his official office was at county headquarters at Milton House, Hawes much preferred the more relaxed and — dare he say it — old-school environment of Mildenheath. As such, he'd retained an office there too, and tended to spend more time there than he did at Milton House.

Jack knew Hawes was one of the only reasons why Mildenheath CID still existed — and why he still had a job — and he also knew the two of them were the sole remaining members of the old guard. Once they were gone — once the others had found a way to get rid of them — Mildenheath CID would close and everything would move into the shiny office headquarters. The death of real policing, Jack used to call it.

'Afternoon, Jack,' Hawes said, his mixed northern accent not having been tempered by years living in and around Mildenheath. 'You're not going to like this, I'm afraid.'

'I had a feeling that might be the case. When was the last time you brought me good news?'

'The new PCC wants to see you. I told her you were out, but she's waiting in my office. I think we both know the sort of thing that's going to crop up, so I just wanted to let you know I'm on your side. You know that.'

He did know that, but he also knew that one of the few responsibilities and powers the Police and Crime Commissioner had was to hire and fire the Chief Constable.

Jack, like many police officers, wasn't a fan of Police and Crime Commissioners. Rather than being experienced police officers or people with any sort of knowledge of policing, they were elected politicians, usually standing under the banner of a major political party and almost always with no policing experience whatsoever.

He'd been particularly unkeen on the previous PCC, Martin Cummings, who'd originally been planning to stand for reelection once his term was up, but who'd had to stand aside following the discovery of some information which could have ruined his career overnight.

It was feared that Cummings would lose to Penny Andrews anyway, and her subsequent election had caused no great surprise — but plenty of consternation — throughout the county's police force.

Penny Andrews was, again, a career politician standing under the banner of a major political party. What upset most police officers was that her party was the current party of government, and one which had based much of its offering on providing a secure and stable police force and greater national security — all whilst slashing police and security budgets at every conceivable point.

The county was already the most underfunded police force in Britain, and that was only going to get worse with Andrews and her cronies in charge.

'Do I have much choice?' Culverhouse asked Hawes.

'Apparently not. She came marching in like she owned the place, going on about how Mildenheath's been run, asking questions about why we felt we were so high and mighty that we didn't need to follow the same rules as everyone else.'

'So why does she want to see me?'

Hawes shuffled uncomfortably. 'I told her *one* of the reasons was that we had an incredibly successful major incident team here, and that Mildenheath posed a number of unique challenges which meant that it was prudent to ensure a dedicated local CID was based in the town.'

Culverhouse raised his eyebrows. 'Maybe you should go into politics yourself. You've got the patter down to a T.'

Hawes let out a small laugh. 'No fear of that, let me tell you. My retirement's going to be filled with nothing but Horlicks and golf.'

'Speaking of which, don't suppose you've got your clubs on you, have you?'

'Now now, Jack. There'll be no assaulting politicians on my watch. At least wait until I've gone home first.'

The two made their way to Hawes's office to find Penny Andrews — the dictionary definition of a power dresser — sitting, waiting for them.

'You must be Detective Chief Inspector Culverhouse. Pleasure to meet you.'

'Hello,' Jack said, not returning the compliment.

'The Chief Constable's been telling me all about you.'

'Really? I hope he mentioned my hot stone massages.'

Andrews looked at them both, displaying perfectly in that moment that she had absolutely no sense of humour whatsoever.

'It was a joke,' Culverhouse said. 'An ice breaker.' He could see he'd have a lot of ice to break.

'Sorry, I don't do ice breakers,' Andrews said. 'I do action. But first I want to find out a little more about you and your team. You're the only satellite criminal investigation department in the county, I believe?'

'That's correct.'

'And the Chief Constable was telling me that there are

some pretty compelling reasons for things to stay that way. Can you tell me what those are?'

Culverhouse ground his teeth, took a deep breath and let it out. 'Let's just say it's a town with a unique set of challenges. We get a lot of violent crime, a higher than average murder rate and we're right on the edge of the county, a long way from Milton House.'

'Policing's going regional, though. Most stuff's not even being done at county level any more, but with multiple forces combining and sharing resources. It's a bit odd for a *town* to have its own police force, isn't it?'

'With respect, we haven't got our own police force. We've got our own police station, like many towns have.'

'Yes, for enquiries and local issues. Not for CID and major incidents. That's almost always dealt with at county or regional level.'

'Yes. *Almost* always. But our local issues are murder and violent crime. And we've got an excellent result rate when it comes to solving those and getting successful prosecutions.'

'Yes, I noticed,' Andrews said, peering over her glasses at some papers in her leather folder. 'Serial killings, child sex gangs, corrupt ex-officers. It's a lot to deal with on your own with such a small team, isn't it?'

Culverhouse shuffled awkwardly in his chair. 'We cope perfectly well. More than perfectly well. Like I say, our success rate speaks for itself.'

'Perhaps so, but I can't say I've yet seen any evidence

that those cases couldn't be dealt with at county or regional level. What on earth makes you think that the same officers couldn't solve the same crimes from Milton House rather than Mildenheath?'

Culverhouse let out a sigh. 'You're not from round here, are you?'

'No, I'm from Sussex.'

'So I hear. I really don't mean to be rude, but there is no way you can understand the nuances and issues we have to deal with at a local level if you're not from the area. Even half the people at the other end of the county don't get it.'

'Oh, I get it. I get it alright,' Andrews said, raising her voice. 'I get that you've got a cushy little number here, running your own team with its own rules, with no organisational structure to speak of. No constant pressure from Superintendents. A Chief Constable who shouldn't even be here but who hangs around Mildenheath like your guardian angel. Don't you worry, I get it.'

'It's called policing. It's that thing we've all been doing for the past couple of decades while you've been trying — and failing — to become an MP. And let's face it, that's the only reason you're here, isn't it? Because even your own party don't think highly enough of you to put you up in a safe seat, so you've had to resign yourself to picking up a fat wad of cash pissing off the police in a different way. Don't you worry, I get it.'

Andrews pursed her lips, narrowed her eyes and stood up without once taking her eyes off of Jack.

'I think that'll be all,' she said quietly. 'Thank you for your time, gentlemen.'

With that, she spun on her stiletto heel and walked out of the office.

Jack smiled and looked at the Chief Constable. 'I think that went well.'

10

Wendy unlocked her front door, dumped her bag by the shoe cupboard and walked through into her kitchen.

'Curry or Chinese?' Xav said, holding two takeaway menus up in the air. 'And before you ask, no, I'm not cooking.'

'I wouldn't want you to,' she said, putting her arms around his waist and kissing him.

'Oh, charming.'

Wendy laughed. 'What I meant was I'd rather we got to spend the evening together, relaxing. It's no fun if one of us is stuck in the kitchen. We might as well make the most of it.'

Xav raised his eyebrows. 'Oh yeah?'

She punched him playfully on the arm. 'You'll be lucky. Especially if you conk out in front of the telly at half eight again.'

'I'll have you know I was merely closing my eyes.'

'And snoring.'

'Breathing heavily.'

'Call it whatever you want. I liked it. Just watching you sitting there with your eyes closed. You looked...'

'Chinese.'

'Sorry?'

'Dinner tonight,' Xav said, holding the Chinese take-away menu aloft and plopping the Indian menu back down on the work surface. 'What do you want?'

'How about a bit of everything?' Wendy said, putting her arms back around his waist and kissing him.

'Well that does sound like a plan... Good day at work, was it?'

'Why do you ask?'

'Because you've got that confident swagger you only get when you've had a good result.'

Wendy smiled at him. 'Then you don't know me as well as you thought you did, do you? Maybe I'm capable of a confident swagger all the time.'

'I certainly won't complain about that,' Xav said. 'So why don't you go and swagger on upstairs and slip into something more comfortable while I get dinner ordered?'

She didn't need asking twice. It was difficult enough to separate her work and home lives as it was, without having to spend the evening sitting around in her work clothes.

She'd made much more of an effort since meeting and becoming serious with Xav, having previously had no issues at all lounging around in her work clothes after a shift — or, if fancy took her, relaxing in her pyjamas in front of the TV. It wasn't that she didn't feel comfortable doing the same thing in front of Xav; she just wanted to make an extra effort for him. Thankfully, she was starting to realise that he was actually a pretty good guy and that her reluctance to get more serious with him had been because of her own hangups.

The past was all a distant memory, though, as she stepped under the shower head and let the hot jets of water wash over her. It was therapeutic, like rinsing off the day's physical and emotional dirt, washing the horrendous crimes and even more horrendous people down the plughole.

It was all part of her transition — the transition from Work Wendy into Home Wendy. From Old Wendy to New Wendy.

his work. He thought the word 'workaholic' was a rather odd one. It seemed to imply he was overly keen on his work, but the fact was he found it a necessary evil. Policing was all he'd ever known. It wasn't the same job as it was when he first started, but he knew that the moment he retired that would be the final nail in the coffin for the old guard of Mildenheath Police. In many ways, it was sheer bloody mindedness that kept him going and stopped him from cashing in his pension.

Before long, though, he wouldn't have much choice. Retirement would be imposed upon him and that would be that. He was never quite sure why largely office-based detectives needed to have an expiry date put on them. More often than not, the experience counted for a huge amount when it came to running a murder investigation. The fact that the police were actively fast tracking university graduates into high-level CID roles was something that worried him deeply. Policing wasn't the sort of thing that could be learned with a university degree, and running a major incident team was definitely something best learned through experience rather than in the classroom.

'That you?' a voice called, pulling him from his reverie. It was Emily, his daughter.

'Yeah, sorry.'

'What for?' she said, appearing in the doorway from the living room.

Jack thought for a moment, then smiled. 'Dunno. Force of habit.'

11

Jack Culverhouse returned home around an hour later, unsure if Emily would be home or not.

His daughter tended to come and go as she pleased. This wasn't something Jack was happy about, but he knew he had to give her her own space. She'd had a difficult upbringing, having been effectively kidnapped by her own mother and dumped on her grandparents, who'd brought her up — unknown to Jack — barely a few miles up the road.

But that was all history. It was water under the bridge. Now all Jack was focused on was building a relationship with his daughter and putting a stop to the loneliness he hadn't even realised had been affecting him for so many years.

After Helen had left, he'd thrown himself heavily into

'Well stop it. You're worrying me. I don't want you turning all soppy. I'll think you're ill or something.'

The growth he'd witnessed in his daughter in a relatively short period of time was incredible. She'd really grown as a young woman in the past year or so, and it was hard to believe she was not even sixteen. It was almost as if being back home with Jack had meant she could finally grow up, finally move on and leave her childhood in the past and become the woman she was always meant to be.

Jack didn't take much credit for that transformation. He couldn't. He hadn't been there. But he'd taken her back in and given her the time and space to grow of her own accord. All due credit had to go straight to Emily.

That's not to say there weren't worries and concerns on Jack's part. He'd seen the scars — historic and fresh — on her forearms and had so far chosen not to say anything. Their relationship hadn't been stable enough, and he certainly didn't want to scare her off just yet. But as their relationship grew, so did his confidence, and he'd told himself he'd keep a close eye and bring the subject up if it seemed that more fresh scars were appearing. It had been a while since they had, though, and Jack comforted himself in the knowledge that Emily was clearly in a much happier place now than she had been. There was no way in hell he wanted to rock that boat.

'Chrissie's coming over for a bit,' he said. 'If that's alright.'

Emily just shrugged. 'Yeah. I'll keep out of the way.'

'You don't have to.'

'I know. But it'll give you some space. I've got home-work to do anyway.'

Jack didn't know of many fifteen-year-olds who'd volun-tarily choose to do their homework on a Saturday night, and he wondered whether it was a story designed to get back to Chrissie, who also happened to be the headteacher of the school Emily attended.

Jack had wished he'd known that when he'd met Chrissie, as the unfortunate coincidence had initially caused some friction with Emily. She claimed it wasn't an issue any more, though, and had actively conspired to ensure the two got together. Sometimes, Jack just couldn't predict what his daughter was going to do. Like her mother, she was spontaneous and unpredictable — something Jack had trouble dealing with at times, being the routine-led homebird he was.

'Em,' he said softly, waiting for her to look at him. 'Are you sure you're alright with this? The Chrissie thing, I mean. I know it's a bit weird for you.'

She shrugged. 'It's not. It was just a surprise at first. Anyway, it's not like you're getting married or anything.'

Emily had a point. He and Chrissie had only spent a handful of evenings together. They'd been for a few meals, met for drinks in a local pub and she'd occasionally popped over to spend the evening watching something on the telly with a bottle of wine. It was nothing serious. For Jack, it was companionship. Chrissie hadn't made any attempt to push him any further, so she was either a really good person who knew not to put pressure on him to move any faster than he was willing to, or she just wasn't that into him.

Either way, he was happy as things were. He had no intention to dive into anything serious and he definitely wasn't going to get married again. That hadn't worked out brilliantly the first time, and he had a slight issue in that he was still technically — and legally — married to Helen. He hadn't wanted to bring up the subject of a divorce, largely as he suspected Helen wouldn't respond brilliantly to the idea. And anyway, what was the point? He had no real need or reason to push divorce proceedings. Their money had always been kept separate, and in a divorce she'd be entitled to claim half of his. The situation wasn't ideal, but sometimes it was better just to let sleeping dogs lie.

'Would it be a problem if we did?' he asked Emily.

Her eyes narrowed. 'What, get married?'

'Yeah.' He didn't know why he'd said this, but it seemed like a good way to gauge Emily's instinctive reaction and see how much of her not caring was just an act.

She looked away and shrugged. 'Dunno. I've not really thought about it. Why? Are you?'

'No. We're not. You don't have to worry about that.'

'Right. Is anything wrong Dad?'

Jack cocked his head slightly. 'Wrong? How do you mean?'

'You've just been really weird lately. Asking weird stuff.'

'It's just dad stuff. At least I thought it was. I'm still learning, don't forget.'

Emily let out a small laugh. 'I know you are. And it's hilarious sometimes.'

12

Elsie Fogg put the bracelet back in the cabinet and let out a small sigh. It had been another quiet day. They were all quiet, these days.

As the proprietor of a mid-market jewellery shop, she felt as if she'd been squeezed from all angles for years. The fashion for cheap costume jewellery had pinched hard, as had the rise of online shopping. And with two major mid-market jewellery chains already in the centre of Milden-heath, she'd relied on locals preferring to buy from her inde-pendent shop, but it was almost impossible to compete.

The truth was she should have given up long ago. She'd wanted to. In any other situation she probably would have done, but this shop had been her mother's before her, and she felt a sense of duty to stick it out to the last. The captain must go down with his ship. In any case, she had no choice as there was no lifeboat. This shop was all she'd ever known.

Her son, Chris, had told her for years she should just close the shop and retire. It'd mean being able to spend more time with him and her grandson, Alfie. But the longer she went on, the harder it was to get out. She already had nothing. She worked in the shop six days a week — and had even tried opening on Sundays to pick up the trade the chains were losing — just to try and claw back some money. But every month she sunk deeper into the red, like a gambler chasing a heavy loss.

Anyway, some things were more important than money.

She straightened her back, feeling the vertebrae crack and pop as she did so, then pulled a vape from the pocket of her cardigan. She pressed the button to heat it, then took a strong, deep drag. Blueberry and cardamom for the end of a day, always.

The second button she pressed was the one which started the roller shutters moving outside the front of the shop, protecting the windows and stock from the local hoodlums. Her mother hadn't needed to worry about that in her day. Wouldn't have even needed to lock the door, probably. Could have just left it open.

Just as she was going for another cheeky drag of blueberry and cardamom, she heard a noise coming from the back of the shop.

It was probably nothing, she told herself. Just the girls

from Superdrug putting the cardboard out for collection. She took out her vape and inhaled deeply, almost choking as the office door burst open and she came face-to-face with two balaclava-clad men.

They were shouting at her, but she couldn't understand a word they were saying. It was just noise. English noise, but noise all the same.

Time seemed to slow down. The noise seemed to go quiet, and all she noticed was one man pointing a shotgun at her while the other went to town on the glass cabinets with a hammer.

The first noise she heard breaking the silence was her own piercing scream. The man with the shotgun grabbed hold of her and clamped his hand over her mouth, leaving her struggling for breath.

It was then that she noticed another two men had entered the shop, and were now spraying a black tarry substance over the security cameras. Elsie wanted to tell them there was no point. They hadn't worked for months. The nice man wanted two hundred quid to get them working again, and that was money she didn't have.

She watched on helplessly as the men emptied the display cabinets, filling two suitcases with as much as they could get their hands on — which was largely made up of broken glass.

An overwhelming sense of anger and betrayal washed over her. She wasn't scared. She was furious.

This was what her mother had worked her fingers to

the bone for. It was what Elsie had dedicated her life to maintaining — the memory of her mother. Fogg's was a Mildenheath institution, and these scrawny little fuckers weren't going to be the ones to consign it to history.

The other three men zipped up the suitcases and made to leave, at which point the man who'd had his hand over Elsie's mouth let go and moved to follow them.

Elsie grabbed hold of his arm, knowing she had to either get a good look at his face or come away with some sort of evidence that could make sure these bastards got caught.

The man shrugged her off, but she was determined. There was no way she was letting go now.

She heard the grunt as he tried to wriggle free, but she didn't see him throw his elbow out behind him, didn't see it careering towards her face.

Elsie tasted the blood before she felt anything, other than the ringing in her ears. She stumbled backwards, trying to stay on her feet, desperate to cling onto her assailant. Before she realised what was happening, her feet had disappeared from under her.

The last sound she heard was the crack as her skull bounced off the corner of a display cabinet. Her last thought was that she hoped her mother would have been proud.

13

Much of policing was about spotting patterns. Indeed, entire computer systems had been designed to analyse cases from police forces right across the country and try to identify any patterns which might arise.

More often than not, though, it was police officers themselves who spotted them, and Jack Culverhouse considered this to be one of his strengths.

Last night's robbery at Fogg's had resulted in the death of the shop's proprietor, and was therefore now being treated as a murder investigation. The pressure from above had been to move the case to Milton House, citing the existing workload on the Mildenheath team. Jack, however, was unrepentant.

He despised having cases taken away from him. Like any job, there were times when it was busier than others. This was no different. He knew his team were more than capable of working on both cases. Besides which, he wasn't entirely convinced they were two separate cases.

Armed robberies were rare in Mildenheath anyway, so that was the first thing that aroused Jack's suspicions. But there was more.

Preliminary investigations had discovered that the weak point at Fogg's was the back door. Somehow the robbers had managed to remove the door with relative ease.

Although the CCTV system in the shop wasn't operating at the time of the robbery, the intruders had tampered with every single camera — even the ones which were well hidden. They were either under the impression that the cameras were working, or they just didn't want to take any chances.

'We've got officers in the shop as we speak, trying to ascertain what's been taken and what's been left,' Jack said, addressing his team at the morning briefing. 'They're a long way from coming to any conclusions, but the old lady's record keeping was good so they've got high hopes. The only thing they can say at the moment is it looks like it was a targeted attack. Debbie, you've got more on this, haven't you?'

'A little,' Debbie said. Feedback from the scene is that not all the display cabinets were broken. Only some of them. They weren't all next to each other, either, so it looks on the face of it as if they knew exactly which ones to go for. I wouldn't be surprised if we find out they were the most valuable items.'

Jack nodded, having assumed much the same himself. 'Steve, did you and Frank manage to find anything on CCTV? Any BMW drivers by any chance?'

'Nothing,' Steve said. 'CCTV round the back's crap. There's a tree in the way. We'd have to look wider. Town centre cameras, maybe some residential if there's anything about.'

'Right. Widen out the timeframes, too. The robbers clearly know the area well. Let's look at the weeks leading up to the robbery. There'll have been someone staking the place out, I'm sure of it. Keep an extra eye out for dark BMWs coming and going. You and Frank prioritise that. Where is the fat fuck anyway?'

'Hospital, guv. His missus has done her knee in again.'

'Jesus Christ. She can't have many left.'

'Fell in the kitchen, apparently. Something to do with complications after her operation.'

Jack vaguely recalled Frank talking about his wife having had a knee replacement, but it hadn't really been the most scintillating of conversations — not that any which involved Frank ever were.

'Well let's hope she's back doing the jive before too long, else we're in grave danger of finding ourselves short-staffed. Any word back yet on cause of death for the old woman? Other than having half her head caved in by the side of a jewellery cabinet.'

'I think we can safely say that's going to be what comes back,' Wendy said. 'They're pretty sure that's what happened. Bearing in mind they went in armed and smashed up the cabinets with some sorts of weapons, if they'd really wanted to cause her some harm they would have used those. Bouncing her head off a cupboard's an odd way to go about it.'

Culverhouse nodded. 'Agreed. I don't imagine they meant to kill her. Maybe she put up a fight. Maybe she tripped. Either way, they've fucked up big time.'

The team all knew what this meant. Far from being a small series of armed robberies, this was now a fully-fledged murder investigation.

14

Later that day, Jack received a call from the front desk to say a man had turned up and wanted to speak to someone about the petrol station robberies.

There'd been some appeal messages posted on social media and local news websites in the hope of finding witnesses. A few calls had come in and were being looked at, but no-one had yet taken it upon themselves to just turn up at the station.

Jack had said he'd come down and speak to him. If it was going to be useful, it was best that it went straight to him. If it was a time waster, Jack would be the best person to get him to fuck off pretty quickly.

He made his way down to the front desk and introduced himself to the only person in the waiting area.

'Hi. Dwayne,' the man said, although Culverhouse would barely have called him a man. He'd put him somewhere between eighteen and twenty-two, built like a broken beanpole with long, greasy hair that stuck to his face where it'd slipped from its ponytail.

'Dwayne...?'

'Yeah. Dwayne.'

Culverhouse looked at him for a moment. 'Your surname.'

'Oh. No, that's my first name.'

'Sorry, did you come here on a fucking windup or something?'

Dwayne's eyes narrowed in confusion. 'No. I walked.'

Culverhouse let out a long sigh and rubbed the bridge of his nose. 'Dwayne, I'm going to make this remarkably simple, even for you. What is your surname?'

'Oh. Etherington-Smythe.'

'Of course. What else? Follow me.'

The pair went through to a small, informal interview room where their conversation could be recorded without Jack having to take down copious notes and write up a formal statement for Dwayne to sign. In any case, he was pretty sure the lad would have enough trouble spelling his first name, never mind his surname.

He sat Dwayne down, ran him through the process and made sure he was relaxed, although he suspected Dwayne had never been anything other than relaxed in his life.

'So, can I have your full name please, Dwayne. Including any middle names.'

'Yeah, it's Dwayne Archibald Randolph Brian Gary Etherington-Smythe.'

'Archibald Randolph Brian Gary?' Culverhouse asked, making sure he'd got them all.

'Yeah. Me Dad was posher than me mum.'

Culverhouse raised his eyebrows and nodded. 'Quite the multicultural citizen, Dwayne. I'm told you wanted to speak to someone about some evidence you have regarding the recent armed robberies at petrol stations in and around Mildenheath?'

'Yeah.'

Culverhouse waited a few moments, then raised his eyebrows again. 'Go on.'

'Well I saw something in the news saying you wanted information on the petrol stations what got done over.'

'Yes,' Culverhouse said, blinking furiously and trying to hold onto his temper.

'So I've come here to speak to you about it.'

Culverhouse took a deep breath. 'What's your connection with the petrol stations?'

'Oh, I used to work at one of them.'

'Which one?'

'Chancel Street.'

'Alright. And how long ago was this?'

Dwayne sat back in his chair forcefully enough that he bounced a little, then crossed his arms. 'Blimey. Must be fifteen years ago now.'

Culverhouse eyed the man carefully. 'How old are you?'

'Me? Thirty-nine.'

'You're thirty-nine?'

'Yeah. Forty next month.'

At that moment, Culverhouse couldn't have been more surprised if Dwayne Etherington-Smythe had told him he was the secret lovechild of Demis Roussos and Barry Gibb.

'You must tell me about your skincare regime, Dwayne. It's clearly working wonders for you.'

'Well, first thing in the morning I put on a—'

'Is there something about the petrol station that made you want to come and make a statement today?'

Dwayne shrugged. 'Not really. Just heard you was looking for people who knew it.'

'Yes. We were kind of hoping for a bit more information, to be honest. Perhaps something that might help us find the robbers.'

'Ah. Well I can't help you there, I'm afraid. I only worked there six weeks.'

There was nothing Culverhouse wanted more in that moment than to ram Dwayne's head through the door.

'What about security measures? CCTV cameras, procedures put in place in case of a robbery, that sort of thing?'

Dwayne shrugged again. 'Dunno nothing about that.'

'Right. So you came all the way down here to tell us

that you worked at one of the petrol stations for six weeks fifteen years ago and don't remember anything about it.'

'That's right, yeah.'

Culverhouse forced a smile. 'Right. We'll be in touch.'

He felt mentally drained as he left the room and decided instead to head out to buy a strong coffee. The machine in the office was getting worse by the day, and was now at the stage where it was spewing out liquid that tasted like cat piss and didn't look much different either.

Fortunately for him, a new coffee shop had opened just across the road from the station, which saved him having to walk fifty yards to the next of Mildenheath's many coffee shops.

He'd only been in there once in the fortnight it had been open, but the young woman behind the counter remembered him immediately. 'Straight black?' she said, trying not to let the tremor in her voice show. She could still remember the last time he came in, where he kept on barking 'Black' over the list of macchiatos, frappes and cappuccinos she was reading out for him.

As far as Culverhouse was concerned, there were only two types of coffee: black or white. And white was for girls.

Once the large black coffee was in his hand, he made his way back across the road and into the station, before heading back to the incident room.

'Guv,' Steve said, the second Culverhouse opened the door.

'What?' came the barked reply.

'We started looking at the CCTV coverage, like you said. We already had the footage from Fogg's as it was seized by officers at the scene, so we thought we'd kick things off there.'

'Wait. I thought the cameras in the shop weren't working?'

'So did we. One of them was working fine, though. It was up high, behind the till counter, facing the door. Perfect location, really.'

'Not for identifying the bastards who came in through the back.'

'Well, no. I was going to come onto that. We've got no faces or anything from the time of the robbery itself. Two backs of heads — or balaclavas, I should say — but that's about it. But we used the footage from that camera to pick up anyone who actually came into the shop and spent some time there in the days before the robbery, especially as the robbers seemed to know where all the best gear was. Pretty easy job, as it happens, seeing as no bugger hardly ever goes in there. There's maybe two or three a day, if that. Footage only goes back a week, but one of the first things we came across was pretty interesting, to say the least. It seems the shop had a visitor.'

'Are you going to spit it out or what, Steve?'

Steve curled his finger to beckon Culverhouse to follow him, which he did. And there, on Steve's computer screen, was a crystal clear picture of Damian King.

15

Wendy Knight had never usually been the sort of person who relished the thought of a night in front of the telly, but she couldn't deny that her thoughts on the matter had changed recently.

The way she thought about many things had changed. She'd become more homely — that was without doubt. The only difficulty was in working out whether her relationship with Xav was the cause or the effect. Was coming home to him making the evenings feel cosier and more intimate, or was she feeling close to him because she'd turned a corner and started to value home life over work?

It was a balance she'd struggled with for a while, and she certainly wasn't alone on that front. It was a universal truth that a huge percentage of police officers had difficulties in their personal lives which were caused either directly or indirectly by the job.

The unpredictable and often late hours caused logistical nightmares, and there were many officers who went days without seeing their own children. Naturally, that put a great strain on many marriages, too. It was undeniable that the job places a huge amount of psychological pressure on people. Officers would put themselves in grave danger on a daily basis for a public who often didn't care. They were abused, assaulted and made to inspect the aftermath of horrific deaths, and got very little out of it other than the average UK salary — if they were lucky. Once that was put against the number of hours they actually worked in any given week, they were lucky if they earned the National Minimum Wage.

And yet she felt happy. She'd spent a long time agonising over whether or not to push for her inspector's exams and achieve a higher rank, but ultimately she felt she'd now achieved her perfect balance.

Xav had always been pretty good at reading her, and that was apparent again as he kissed her on the head, their eyes not leaving the television, as he spoke softly.

'You seem really happy.'

Wendy smiled. 'I am.'

The TV was showing a documentary about a train accident in Harrow in the 1950s. It was one of those moments where they were both fixed to the screen but neither of them were really watching it — something which was known to both but spoken by neither.

'What's brought that on then?' Xav asked.

'Alright, Mr Low Self Esteem. Or are you just fishing for compliments?'

'Oh, well if I'd known it was all down to me I would've asked much sooner.'

'It isn't.'

'Charming.'

Wendy laughed. 'It's lots of things. And yes, you are one of those things.'

'I've been called worse.'

'I just feel like everything's good. Balanced.'

'How do you mean?'

'In terms of work and home life, I mean.'

'Blimey. Well you must be the first police officer to have managed that, then. You should write a book. Then you could give up the day job altogether.'

Wendy chuckled, and tried to pull her attention back to the documentary. It had been on for a good twenty minutes so far, but she hadn't really taken much notice of it.

Xav, however, seemed a little more distracted. 'I've got to ask,' he said, after a minute or so. 'When you say you're happy as things are, is that your way of saying you don't want to take the inspector's exam after all? I don't mean that negatively. Just asking.'

'No. I just like spending time with you, alright? For the first time in a long time, I'm happy as things are. Even if you are doing your best to make it wear off pretty damn quickly,' she joked.

'I don't think it will.'

'What?'

'Wear off. I think we'll grow and adapt together, whatever happens.'

To Wendy, this seemed like an odd turn of phrase for Xav to use. 'What do you mean?'

Xav pulled away from Wendy and turned to look at her. 'Alright. Would you say I've changed at all in the time you've known me? Grown or adapted?'

'You've certainly not grown up if that's what you mean.'

Xav gave her a look that told her to be serious.

'Honestly? No,' she said. 'You've stayed the same old you the whole way. And that's what I love about you.'

He nodded slowly and sat back in the sofa again, his arm around her.

'Why?' she asked. 'Do you think I've changed?'

'I dunno. I guess we all change to some degree.'

'But I just said you haven't.'

'I know.'

'But I have?'

'Not in a bad way, I don't mean. All I mean is when we first met you were really ambitious and work-focused, and now you've pulled back on that a bit.'

'So?'

'Nothing. I didn't mean it like that. I just meant that I didn't want to be the one who pulled you off track or stopped you achieving your dreams. It's great that you want to be with me and spend so much time with me, but I'd hate to stop you being you.'

'Well you aren't, alright? And anyway, while we're talking about things not changing or moving on, haven't you had any news on your house yet?'

Xav'd had his house on the market for quite some time, but viewings had been sparse and there hadn't yet been any concrete interest from a buyer. Deep down, Wendy suspected there was more to this than met the eye and wondered whether he was secretly trying to hold on to the place rather than committing entirely to her. And it was comments like his a few moments ago which tended to back up that theory.

'Nothing yet. The market's slow at the moment, apparently.'

'Weird.'

'Why's it weird?'

'Because the place across the road was only on the market three days. The new lot move in a week Tuesday.'

'So?'

'So it's virtually identical to yours.'

'It's not even in the same town, Wendy.'

'That's not the point. If that one sold so quickly, why has yours barely had any viewings?'

'Because they probably wanted to live in Mildenheath. My house isn't in Mildenheath. Maybe they were trying to get the kids into a specific school, or be walking distance from work. Give it til a week Tuesday and you can ask them, can't you?'

'Alright. No need to get defensive.'

'I'm not being defensive. I'm just letting you know you're being unreasonable.'

'I think maybe you should change agents.'

'I will do.'

'When?'

Xav made a show of looking at his watch. 'I thought I might just wait for them to open up tomorrow morning rather than camping outside their shop overnight, if that's alright?'

'You can camp out in the back garden if you're going to carry on like that.' *Or go back to* your *place*, Wendy wanted to add.

'Look, can't we just have a nice relaxing evening enjoying our three-pound bottle of plonk and watching hundreds of people die in a horrific train crash?'

'Preferable to speaking to me, is it?' Wendy asked, smiling.

Xav laughed. 'Something like that.'

16

The next morning brought news that Damian King had been arrested and brought in for questioning. Owing to the seriousness of the investigation and Jack's general reluctance to let anyone else have even the smallest amount of control over anything, he'd declared that he and Wendy would be conducting the interview.

Enough time had passed between seeing Damian on CCTV inside Fogg's and him being arrested, which meant they were confident in the questions they'd be asking him.

On the whole, police interviews tended to be far more heavily structured than people thought. Even if the investigation appeared to have a suspect bang to rights, a similar formula was followed each time.

The initial interview was designed to seek basic information, even if far more advanced evidence was already known. This was where they'd ask the suspect where he'd been at the time of the crime, whether there were alibis to that effect, what his connection was. At that point, even if the officers knew for a fact the offender was lying, it was often let go in order to allow the suspect enough rope to hang himself.

The second interview was where the fun kicked in. At that point there'd be a whole host of statements from the suspect they now knew to be demonstrably untrue, and that was the point at which the evidence was unfurled and the suspect's jaw hit the carpet. While they're on the ropes, the officers would piece the evidence together in front of the suspect and make a representation to them that it was clear they committed the crime and this was their chance to confess.

It was a structure and technique which had proven successful throughout the years, but there were always situations where it was not appropriate. And Jack Culverhouse had to admit he quite liked to use shock tactics at times.

Up until then they'd had very little on Damian King other than his past form, but now they had evidence he'd been in Fogg's just a few days before the robbery. He would have had at least a passing knowledge of what was in each of the cabinets. And, of course, he was linked to Gumbert's chain of petrol stations.

He still didn't think Damian had done the robberies himself — that would be far too risky, even for someone with his mental capacity, which was only marginally above that of an amoeba. But Jack was certain he was involved somewhere along the line. He just had to figure out which piece of the puzzle Damian King was — and who the other pieces were.

Jack started the interview process and ran through the formalities of Damian's previous statement. Again, he'd declined the opportunity to have a solicitor present, somehow believing that this would indicate some level of guilt on his part. Jack and Wendy dearly wanted to let him know how much of a bad idea this was on his part, but were quite content to let him be the architect of his own downfall. It was extraordinary how many suspects had watched a couple of telly programmes and genuinely believed the presence of a solicitor would make them seem guilty. It was akin to thinking having a bank account is an acceptance that you're shit with money, or that taking a train or taxi means you can't drive.

In any case, it wasn't Jack and Wendy's place to tell Damian he was carving out his own shortcut to the Crown Prosecution Service. With any luck the plank would decide to represent himself in court, too.

'Damian, have you ever been to Fogg's jewellers in Mildenheath?' Wendy asked.

'What, ever? In my life?'

'Let's just narrow it down to the last week or so.'

'Don't remember.'

'You don't remember if you visited a jewellery shop in the last week?'

'I get really hazy with my memory,' Damian replied, smirking.

'Maybe this'll jog it,' Culverhouse said, passing a blown-up photograph across the desk. It clearly showed Damian inside Fogg's, looking into a jewellery cabinet. 'Is this you?'

'You tell me.'

'Alright. That's you.'

'If you say so.'

'I just did. What were you doing in there?'

'What, so it's illegal to go in a jewellery shop now is it? I don't remember nothing about that on my parole sheet.'

'What did we arrest you for, Damian?' Wendy asked.

'Dunno, wasn't listening.'

'On suspicion of armed robbery and conspiracy to armed robbery.'

Damian shrugged. 'You can arrest me for all you like. I ain't done nothing wrong.'

Culverhouse leaned forward. 'Ah, now you see, that's just the problem. You might think that's the case, but the law will take a very different view. You're linked to the petrol station robberies by virtue of the fact that you had intimate knowledge of the security systems there. And we know the robbers had that knowledge too. You've got a criminal record for violent conduct and you were let go from the petrol stations for stealing money from the tills. And, whaddya know, a few days before a local jewellery shop is robbed — in which a woman died — you were at the scene. You can protest your innocence all you like, Damian, but it's not looking good, is it?'

Damian swallowed. 'Died?'

'The owner of the shop fell and hit her head in the commotion,' Wendy said. 'She died shortly afterwards.'

Damian's eyes were glassy. 'No. I didn't do nothing. I swear down. Listen, I'll drop the fucking bravado, alright? But you've got to believe me. I've got fuck all to do with them robberies.'

'We're all ears, Damian,' Culverhouse said.

Damian took a deep breath. 'I went in to buy a ring.'

'What kind of ring?'

'An engagement ring,' he replied, his eyes scrunched closed.

'Didn't know you were all loved up, Damian. Tell me more.'

'Do I have to?'

'I'm afraid we're going to need a bit more than that, yes. Forgive me if I'm not inclined to just take your word for it and leave it at that.'

Damian sighed heavily and seemed to be genuinely anguished. 'Look, it's tough being on a tag, alright? Birds ain't exactly lining up to be with me at the moment, so I had to try other things.'

'Such as?'

He swallowed hard. 'I've been going to see this woman. She's... less picky.'

'How do you mean?'

'I mean she's a fucking hooker, don't I?' Damian said, barking through gritted teeth.

Culverhouse had to admit he got more than a slight thrill at seeing Damian so pained and chastened.

'Just so we're clear, you've found that women no longer find you attractive now that you're walking around with an electronic tag on your ankle due to the violent crimes you've committed, so you took to visiting a prostitute as the only means of getting your end away?'

Damian stared at Jack, clearly wanting to explode but knowing he had no other option than to comply. 'Yes. If you want to put it like that.'

'Just a statement of the facts. Where did you get the money from, Damian? Or was she not a very expensive one?'

Damian gritted his teeth. 'I used some of my mum's money.'

'Brave,' Culverhouse said, with a raised eyebrow. 'I'm pretty sure that's not what she meant when she said she was offering you pocket money, but that's a matter between you and her.'

'And you were buying an engagement ring for this woman?' Wendy asked.

'Oh Christ, yeah. I forgot about that bit,' Culverhouse said, smiling. 'That's the cherry on the cake, that one. Tell us more.'

Damian looked down at the floor for a while before

speaking. 'I like her, alright? We get on. She respects me. I just wanted to respect her back.'

'I'm pretty sure that's not for us to comment on, as much as I'd love to,' Culverhouse said. 'Now be a good boy and jot her contact details down here so we can go and speak to her.'

Damian bit his lip, then did as he was told.

Once the interview had been terminated, Jack and Wendy left the room and signalled for an officer to take Damian back to his cell. There was still plenty of time left on the custody clock, and they didn't want to — or have to — risk him doing a runner in the meantime.

'Fuck,' Jack said, slapping his forehead. 'I buggered that right up.'

'Why? What happened?' Wendy asked, suddenly concerned.

'King taking his mum's money to pay for the hooker. Would've been funnier if I'd called it front-pocket money.'

17

Even though it had been clear to Jack and Wendy through Damian's enormous discomfort and embarrassment that he was telling the truth, 'He shuffled a bit awkwardly, m'lud' wasn't something that'd get past a judge. To that effect, Debbie Weston had looked into his claims using the contact details for the prostitute.

Jack, meanwhile, had only felt his frustration grow at Damian King wriggling off the hook for the second time that week, even when it looked as though he was bang to rights. Either Jack was barking up the wrong tree or King wasn't half as daft as he looked. Either way, it infuriated Jack.

'The woman's known to us,' Debbie told Jack in his office, reeling off some of her past offences. 'Nothing much recently, so maybe she's reformed herself.'

'Apart from the prostitution, you mean.'

'Yeah, apart from that.'

'And what about the back door at Fogg's? Did you manage to locate the contractor who fitted it?'

Debbie closed her eyes. 'No. Sorry.'

'Why not?'

'It slipped my mind. I'm sorry.'

'I ask you to make a couple of basic phone calls which could lead us to a gang of armed robbers, and it slipped your fucking mind? It's not good enough.'

'I've got a lot going on at the moment, what with my mum and everything.'

'Well your mum's not on a major incident team, is she? You've just had god knows how long off to go and spend time with her. You've got absolutely no idea what strings I had to pull to get that allowed. So I'd appreciate it if you could at least manage to do some basic fucking work now you're back, alright?'

Debbie said nothing, and left his office.

Half an hour later, there was another knock at the door and Wendy came in.

'What happened with Debbie?' she asked.

'Absolutely fuck all. That's the problem.'

'If I can be honest, I think you need to give her some slack. She's had a tough time of it recently.'

'And if I can be honest, I think you need to fuck off. She's a police officer on a major incident team. We've all got things going on in our personal lives, but we're also experienced enough to know we have to leave that at the door.'

'With respect, you can't keep talking to people like that.'

Jack looked up at her. 'Shut up, Knight.'

'I'm serious. I know you always manage to do it in your own dry, jokey way. And I know we're all used to it. But sometimes there'll be someone who's not in the right place to take it quite so casually. And I think bearing in mind what Debbie's going through, she's probably one of those at the moment.'

'She can handle it,' Jack replied. 'She's been through worse. Was that everything, Detective Sergeant Knight?'

Wendy looked at him for a moment. 'Actually, no. I wanted to let you know that I took it upon myself to look into the company who fitted the door. We've got a name.'

'What? How?'

'I sent Ryan down to see if there was any paperwork in the shop's office. While I was busy consoling Debbie, that is.'

'What, inside half an hour? How did she even gain entry?'

'She didn't need to. There was a sticker on the door, proudly declaring it had been fitted by Supreme Locks & Glazing. So I did a bit of digging and looked up Supreme Locks & Glazing at Companies House to see who the director was.'

'And?'

Wendy took a sheet of printed paper out of her pocket, unfolded it and placed it in front of Jack, watching a smile spread across his face.

He looked up at her. 'Got him. We've got the fucker.'

18

Jack Culverhouse was grinning like the Cheshire Cat as he marched through into the main incident room and began to address his team.

'Ladies and gentlemen. And you, Ryan. Detective Sergeant Knight has just come to me with a piece of information I'm sure you're all going to find just as exciting as I am. If you don't, please at least pretend you do. In short, it appears that the company who fitted the back door at Fogg's jewellers — the back door which was so easily breached, and whose security measures seem to have been fed to the robbers — is owned by one Gary McCann.'

A small ripple of noise ran through the room as the realisation of what this meant became apparent. Culverhouse and his team had been trying to pin crimes on McCann for years, but he had always proved to be a slippery customer. There was no doubt amongst the police — or the residents of Mildenheath in general — that McCann had devoted himself to a life of crime, but they had never been able to prove anything.

His name had surfaced time and time again in connection with various major crimes which had passed through their office. It had often got to the point where Jack would automatically assume that any difficult-to-solve case must automatically have McCann's name on it, and he had often been proved wrong — much to his chagrin.

McCann had made no secret of having enjoyed watching Culverhouse and his team get slapped down on numerous occasions, keeping quietly confident as accusation after accusation was levelled at him before being batted away with ease.

The truth was McCann had fingers in lots of pies, many of them unsavoury. He was known locally as a businessman who specialised in rescuing struggling companies. He'd buy the owners out, relieve them of their business debts and keep them on as employees. That was the official line, anyway. The rumour — although never proven — was that he did this for one of two reasons. Either he had a use for the person whose loyalty he'd just bought, or he needed another avenue to launder the money from his less legal enterprises.

'I want everything thrown at investigating Supreme Locks & Glazing and McCann himself,' Culverhouse said.

'He won't actually run the company himself, though. He might be listed as the owner, but it's not like he's going

to be going out with his jemmy and a can of WD-40, is it?'
Steve Wing said, chuckling to himself.

'No, but it's definite link, Steve,' Culverhouse replied.
'If his company fitted the door, they'd know about the security weaknesses. They'd know how to get in.'

'Doesn't it sound a bit tenuous, though?' Frank Vine
asked.

'Big word for you, Frank,' came Culverhouse's terse
reply.

'Very funny. But think about it. Gary McCann's got a
stake in god knows how many businesses around here. His
name's bound to crop up at some point. It always does. And
how many times have we spent man hours chasing leads to
do with him, only to find out we've been barking up the
wrong tree?'

Before Culverhouse could answer, Debbie Weston
chipped in, seemingly buoyed by not being the only person
to speak out against him.

'It's entirely up to you, sir, and I agree it's something we
need to look into, but I don't think throwing everything at
this particular lead's going to do us any good.'

'Right. And when you're the senior investigating officer,
you can decide what's going to do us good. Until then, that's
my responsibility.'

'Oh, come off it. You're just pissed off that all your other
leads have dried up. You're grasping at straws, and this one
fell into your lap because you've had a grudge against
McCann for years.'

He looked at Debbie, unsure whether to be angered at her answering him back or impressed that she'd actually stood up for herself for once. Either way, she'd acted heavily out of character.

'Alright. Let's make this democratic, shall we? How about one of you comes up with a better idea? Why don't you let me know about all the much stronger leads you've managed to generate? No? Nothing? Well in that case you'd better investigate the one lead we do have, hadn't you? Because if we don't — if this one gets away from us — that Andrews woman is going to have plenty of fucking reasons to move you lot up to Milton House, right under Malcolm Pope's snotty nostrils. And believe you me, I will not be going with you.'

Culverhouse didn't want a response, and he didn't wait for one. Instead, he turned and left.

19

Jack'd had just about enough of this day. It was one of those where he knew nothing was going to go right for him, and he was already thinking about how to spend his evening. He knew exactly what he'd like to do, and he had a good feeling he might be successful in this regard, at least.

He paced down the corridor, listening as the phone rang, waiting for Chrissie to answer. There was a good chance she wouldn't, especially if she was in a meeting, but Jack hated text messages. If she was tied up, she'd see the missed call and ring him back later.

Just as he was about to hang up the phone, it connected and Chrissie answered.

'Reporting for detention, miss,' he joked. The local-school-headteacher jokes were starting to run a bit thin, but Jack reckoned he had a few left in his arsenal yet.

'As long as it's not an after-school detention, I don't

mind,' Chrissie said. 'I've had it up to here today, and I don't intend on staying a minute later than I need to.'

'That is music to my ears. What does miss say to a cheeky bottle of vino behind the bike sheds?'

'Looks like it's going to rain, unfortunately.'

'Never mind. Have to be at mine, then, won't it?'

'And do you have a warrant, Detective Chief Inspector?'

'Do I need one?'

Chrissie chuckled. 'I reserve the right to remain silent.'

'That's what the yanks say. Over here we warn you that it may be held against you.'

'Now you're talking.'

Jack smiled and felt a small flutter. It had been a while since he'd been able to have this sort of flirtatious conversation with anyone. His wife, Helen, hadn't been a particularly flirty woman either. He always hesitated to refer to her as his wife. To all intents and purposes she was his ex-wife, but there had been no divorce proceedings — mainly due to Helen's penchant for disappearing without trace for months and years at a time.

'Just promise me one thing,' he said to Chrissie.

'Name it.'

'None of that cheap French shit, alright?'

'Are we talking about my wine or your aftershave, Detective Chief Inspector?'

'Touché. I tell you what. You lay off the Blue Nun and I'll go easy on the Lynx Africa. Deal?'

Chrissie laughed again. 'And which one are we meant to be drinking?'

'Close call. We'll toss a coin.'

'How does eight o'clock sound?'

'Is that the earliest you can do?' he asked, hoping he didn't have to wait that long.

'That all depends on whether you want me wearing my best face and having sourced the finest wine for sir.'

'Let's call it seven and we'll pass on the face.'

Spotting Wendy approaching him in the corridor, Jack said his goodbyes and ended the call.

'News?' she asked.

'No, it was Chrissie.'

Wendy nodded. 'What did you say you're going to do on her face?'

'Long story. What's up?'

'Probably nothing, but just something that I spotted and which I thought might be worth mentioning. It's silly, but I'd feel worse if I didn't point it out.'

'What is it now?'

'The petrol station robberies and the incident at Fogg's. There's something else that links them. Someone who knew about the lack of security measures in all those locations.'

'Who?'

Wendy swallowed. 'I don't think you're going to like this.'

20

Jack let out a long breath as his jaw tightened. 'You have no idea what a can of fucking worms that would open, Knight.'

'Trust me, I do. But we can't just ignore it. PC Curwood was on the Safer Communities scheme designed to push crime prevention. His role was to visit local business premises to give them security advice and help them prevent crime. I've checked the system and he personally visited each of the three petrol stations as well as Fogg's jewellers.'

'For Christ's sake, he's one of ours. If he was on that scheme he'll have visited dozens of business premises in the area. Hundreds, probably. Using that logic, you might as well arrest the postman as well.'

'We've still got to look into it. I know it's not convenient, but it's entirely possible.'

'Not convenient? Are you having a laugh? Do you have

any idea what sort of process this kicks off? It'd mean getting Professional Standards involved, having every little thing we do scrutinised, putting us in the firing line and giving Penny fucking Andrews yet another reason to shut us down.'

'With respect, if we've got a corrupt officer on the streets, there are bigger problems to worry about.'

'I'm not sure some daft old bugger getting his shops done over because he keeps his life savings in a shoebox is more important than all of us losing our jobs.'

'That's not really for us to decide, though, is it? And anyway, it's more than that now. Elsie Fogg died because of what happened. What's to say they won't do the same again? What if our lot actually manage to respond to a call on time, meet the robbers head on and one of ours gets hurt? Or worse.'

'You're still under the assumption that you're right. Be very careful about that. We've got absolutely nothing linking PC Curwood to this, other than the fact he's the poor bastard who had to go out and give them security advice. Which, I might add, is his job.'

Wendy shook her head. 'There's more than that. Ryan looked into the records from the Safer Communities visits. Just so we could find out where the weaknesses were, see if we could tie up and links to what happened. She asked me to explain something on the system she didn't understand, and that's when I noticed Theo Curwood's name on each of the site visits. I had a closer look at the records. Despite the fact that we know the petrol stations didn't have working CCTV and kept their week's takings in a bucket underneath the counter, he didn't note any major security concerns. Same goes for Fogg's.'

Culverhouse gritted his teeth and sighed heavily. 'Did you say anything to Ryan?'

'No. I haven't said anything to anyone. I don't even know if I should be saying it to you. One of us needs to speak to Professional Standards.'

'Forget that for now. We need to find out how many premises PC Curwood visited. We know these guys are violent, and they've already killed someone. They're not going to be scared to try it again, so we need to narrow down the potential list of future targets. Christ knows how we'll do that, but it's got to be our main focus.'

'Where would we even start? Even if we only look at the places he visited, there's no way of knowing which ones have weak security. Especially if he's told them all their setup is absolutely fine and that's what it says on the paper-work. If we sent other officers in to do another review of them all it'd take weeks. Not to mention the cost.'

'And potentially tipping PC Curwood off that some-thing's wrong.'

'Exactly. There's nothing we can do on that front. As much as I hate to say it, all we can do is sit back and wait for the next call.'

'No,' he said. 'There has to be something. I'm not having blood on my hands.'

'Like what? We could always ring around the other businesses he visited and mention the fact there's been a spate of armed robberies and they might want to be extra vigilant.'

'And when they tell you it's alright because that nice police officer told them they're safer than Fort Knox? Are you going to tell them a corrupt police officer lied to them in order to make sure they got done over, their businesses were ruined and their lives were put at risk?'

Wendy sighed and leant back against the wall. As much as she wanted to have an answer to that, she didn't.

21

'You know the procedure. It's not my place to tell you, but you're duty bound to contact Professional Standards,' Wendy said.

'You're right. It's not your place to tell me. I'll have a word with this Curwood bloke myself. I can spot a bull-shitter a mile off.'

Wendy tried not to let the frustration show on her face. Jack Culverhouse had always been old-school, but there had been many occasions on which he'd sailed far too close to the wind. It wasn't that he was a rule breaker as a matter of habit, but if those rules got in the way of his intended course of action he had a tendency to bend them ever so slightly.

She'd never been entirely sure how he'd managed to get away with it for so long. There was only so much leeway he could get by simply pointing out that he got results. Lots of police officers got results. But the Chief Constable, Charles Hawes, was cut from much the same cloth as Jack. The only difference with Hawes was that he had been able to keep his actions and opinions in check for long enough to ride the wave of diplomacy to the top. With Hawes now considering retirement, Wendy wondered how long Jack would have left without his guardian angel in charge of Mildenheath Police.

The pressure was on, though. There had been plenty of agitation from the previous Police & Crime Commissioner, Martin Cummings, to close down Mildenheath CID and have it subsumed into county police headquarters at Milton House. Although Cummings was now gone, his replacement, Penny Andrews, seemed even more determined to make her mark with a major reorganisation plan.

Wendy knew that Jack would be gone the second that happened, and the job wouldn't be the same again. Even though she'd always been a stickler for correct procedure, she couldn't deny that working at Mildenheath with its own quirky ways and means had given her a new outlook on the job — and on life. She had to admit she'd miss it if it went.

But there were some pretty clear places that lines were drawn, and police corruption was one of them.

'This will get out,' Wendy told him. 'It'll be uncovered at some point, and they'll find out that you knew and covered it up.'

'And what? I'll get to retire early. What a travesty.'

'Without a pension, and probably with a criminal record in its place.'

Jack seemed to think for a moment, then shook his head. 'I'm not having it. This sort of thing was stamped out years ago. Believe me. I was there. It was all over the place. Every second officer was on the take in one way or another. But not now. No-one's stupid enough to do that now. The background checks are crazy, for a start.'

'Anyone can have their head turned. Especially by money. What if he's been offered a cut of whatever they make from these raids? Think about it. Not only would having Curwood onside mean they're able to gain access to premises with crap security, but they've also got him able to report back about the investigation. He can feed back to them what's going on, what we know, what we don't. And all for a cut of the spoils.'

'And what if that's horseshit?' Jack replied. 'What if he's just crap at his job? What if he was sick and tired of having to go into all these shops and petrol stations, asking the same bloody questions, checking all their locks and security setup? What if he just did the bare minimum and told the owners everything was fine so he could get home and put his feet up in front of Coronation Street?'

'That's for Professional Standards to decide. It's their job to investigate and come to their own conclusions.'

Jack shook his head. 'And subject the guy to that sort of treatment? They'll bug his phone, break into his emails, follow him around. And for what? We don't know he's done anything wrong. He's a police officer, for fuck's sake. Doesn't that count for anything anymore?'

'Everyone needs to be treated equally,' Wendy replied. 'Besides, what's the worst that can happen? Like you say, he could be subjected to undercover surveillance. They might have a look at his texts. So what?'

'Would you like someone snooping through your texts?'

'No, but I've got nothing to hide. I wouldn't like it, but it's better than the alternative — that we do nothing, and we're wrong. Then more businesses get broken into. More people have their livelihoods ransacked and ruined. And what if someone else loses their life in the process? Elsie Fogg might not be the last. Can you live with that on your conscience?'

Jack looked at her. She could see his jaw clenching and unclenching as he ground his teeth. With a hand on one hip, he rubbed his chin with the other hand, rasping it against his stubble.

'I'm going to get another coffee,' he said. 'You coming?'

22

Jack had spent much of the afternoon thinking about the evening. He'd planned to have Chrissie over to his place for a bottle of wine and a bite to eat, but he'd changed his mind. He needed a change of scenery to take his mind off the events of the day, so he'd texted her and asked if she'd like to go out instead. Thankfully, she agreed, so he called Alessandro's and booked a table for two.

Mildenheath wasn't exactly blessed with fine restaurants, and Alessandro's was about as good as it got, which was fine. It was certainly a lot better than any of the burger joints or pub-grub chains that had sprung up across the town over the past couple of decades. There were more upmarket options in the surrounding towns and villages, of course, but tonight needed to be simple and relaxing. No worrying about who was going to drive or trying to order a cab home at the end of the night.

Alessandro's was probably the most romantic of Mildenheath's restaurants, too. Situated downstairs in what used to be a basement underneath — bizarrely enough — an entirely unrelated Italian eatery, it was full of the rustic charm of old Italy and had been a staple of Mildenheath's high street for more than forty years.

The evening had gone exactly to plan, and the pair were relaxing admirably — not something either of them found easy to do under normal circumstances.

'I've got to ask,' he said, when the conversation fell quiet for a moment or two. 'That thing about Miss Thompson and the caretaker...'

Chrissie let out a full belly laugh. 'I wondered how long it was going to take you to ask that. I could see the look on your face when Emily mentioned it god-knows how long ago.'

Jack took the ribbing like a gentleman, then cocked his head. 'And?'

'And it'd be unprofessional of me to confirm or deny those rumours.'

'I looked her up on the school website. She's a bit of a sort, ain't she? Wouldn't surprise me one bit if the caretaker had fancied a piece.'

'Like I said to Emily, it was a vicious rumour. These things tend to fly around in high schools.'

'Yeah, a bit like STDs.'

Chrissie chuckled. 'They're called STIs now, actually.'

'Who caught them?'

'The STIs?'

'No, Miss Thompson and the caretaker.'

Chrissie opened her mouth to answer the question, then stopped herself.

'Got you!' Jack said. 'You were about to tell me.'

'Bullshit.'

'You were. Don't forget it's my job to spot people who are lying to me.'

'And it's my job to help children grow up,' Chrissie replied, winking.

'Alright,' Jack said, raising his hand in a mock scout's salute. 'I promise I won't tell anyone about Miss Thompson shagging the caretaker.'

Chrissie smiled and shook her head, before taking a mouthful of wine.

'And what about you?' Jack asked.

'What about me?'

'Have you ever had any romantic liaisons with a co-worker? Either in the stationery store or not.'

'Definitely not. Very cramped in there,' she replied, smirking.

'But otherwise?'

'It would be highly inappropriate for a headteacher to be romantically or otherwise involved with a teacher at the school,' she said, with a heavy emphasis on her job title.

Jack thought about this for a moment. 'So not while you've been headteacher, then?'

'Like I said, that would be highly inappropriate.'

'But before you became head?'

'I plead the fifth, Detective Chief Inspector.'

'You can't. We're not in America. Come on. Spill.'

Chrissie shrugged coyly. 'I've been in the job a long time. Never married. Plenty of male colleagues. We're around each other for ten hours a day. You know how it is.'

'I promise you I don't. You haven't met my colleagues,' Jack replied, visions of a sweating, naked Steve Wing running through his mind.

'There might have been one or two brief flings. Let's leave it at that.'

Jack could see from the look on Chrissie's face that she wasn't necessarily uncomfortable with the conversation. If anything, she seemed to enjoy teasing him.

'Alright. I'll get you drunk later and ask you again.'

'Ask me all you like, Detective Chief Inspector. A lady never kisses and tells. What about you?'

'What about me?'

'Have you never been tempted to cop off with someone at work? Pardon the pun.'

The vision of Steve returned. 'No. Not in a million years.'

'So what's your dirty secret then?'

'I don't have one.'

'Oh, come on. I've told you mine.'

'No you haven't. You fluttered your eyelashes a bit and told me you didn't want to talk about it.'

'Alright. Three.'

'Three?'

'Three colleagues. Your turn.'

Jack looked at her for a few moments. The way in which she'd casually revealed that information was both unexpected and strangely erotic.

He thought for a second or two, trying to work out if he could come back with something equally playful, but he couldn't. In any case, there was something he needed to tell Chrissie and this seemed like a better time than any.

As he opened his mouth to tell her, he decided against it. At some stage she'd have a right to know he wasn't actually divorced, and that his wife had proven almost impossible to track down. He wanted to tell her. But at the same time he knew he couldn't risk wrecking what he and Chrissie had. She was the first woman who'd taken any interest in him in years. Although he knew she'd likely be absolutely fine with the situation, he wasn't going to take any risks. In any case, things were still fairly casual between them and it wasn't as if they were lining up their own white wedding any time soon.

'I almost got a criminal record when I was younger,' he replied. 'I got caught nicking sweets from the local corner shop. Twice.'

'Twice? Wow. A proper little gangster, weren't you?' Chrissie said, laughing.

'You laugh, but I was fifteen. First time they let me go, second time the owner marched me down to the police station. Fortunately they couldn't be arsed with the paper-work, but I was lucky.'

'Would it have stopped you going into the police force?'

'To be honest, I don't know. I kind of put it behind me after it happened. These days I think you're stuffed if you've ever been given a sentence for anything, or cautioned in the last five years. I tend to try and avoid the recruitment side of things though, so I'm a bit rusty. Too many spotty kids for my liking.'

'You were one once.'

'Yeah. I was. And I got knocked into shape pretty bloody quickly.'

Jack thought briefly about his early days in the police force. He'd certainly been a different officer to the one he was now. He'd been wetter behind the ears, full of promise and optimism. It was strange how the police force managed to squash that out of everyone pretty quickly, even back then.

'Listen,' he said, a combination of reminiscing and a bottle of wine leading him to other thoughts. 'Why don't you come over for dinner one night with me and Emily?'

Chrissie looked at him for a moment. 'Honestly? Will she be okay with that? I mean, I know she's doing a great job of pretending this isn't happening, but wouldn't that be a bit much for her?'

Jack shrugged. 'She'll have to deal with it, won't she? I didn't know you were her headteacher. And anyway, she'll be out of school within a year or so.'

'I was kind of hoping she'd stay on for sixth form.'

'Me too, but I've learned not to try and predict anything Emily's going to do.' His mind's eye wandered to the cuts he'd seen on his daughter's forearms. The ones he'd chosen to ignore.

Chrissie looked at him and smiled. 'Alright then. I'd like that.'

23

Jack felt fortunate that he was due to start work later than usual that morning. One bottle of wine had turned into two, and then three. He didn't often get hangovers, but his body was certainly doing its best to help him regret the previous night's excesses.

He squeezed his eyes hard shut and stretched the muscles in his face as he tried to get the blood flowing to his head, hoping that might go some way to relieving the pounding headache, then got up and sauntered across the landing towards the bathroom.

As he opened the door, the smell of vomit hit him like a tonne of bricks. It was enough to make him feel queasy at the best of times, but his delicate stomach almost lost control as the sharp, acrid smell lodged itself in his lungs.

Holding his breath, he leaned across and opened the

window, swinging it open on its hinges before leaving the bathroom and closing the door. It seemed he hadn't been the only one drinking to excess last night.

He'd often wondered if Emily had been experimenting with drink and drugs while she was out with friends, but he knew from his job that there really was no use in worrying about it. The more pressure parents put on their kids, the more likely they were to rebel. They'd all experiment at some point, and all he could do was make sure she was relatively safe.

He got dressed, then went downstairs for breakfast. He figured he'd use the downstairs loo for now. Brushing his teeth could wait until the smell had dissipated upstairs.

When he reached the kitchen, Emily was already sitting at the table in her dressing gown, her hair looking like she'd been dragged through a hedge backwards, eyes down and concentration entirely on whatever social media website she was browsing on her phone.

'Morning,' he said, alarmed at how gruff his own voice sounded — even by his own standards.

'Hi,' came the delicate reply.

'Good night last night?' he said, trying not to sound too cocky for fear of being questioned about his own alcohol consumption.

'Yeah, was okay.'

'What time did you get in?'

Emily shrugged, barely perceptibly. 'Dunno. Elevenish.'

Jack knew that wasn't true, as he was still up at ten to midnight himself. He knew when to pick his battles, though, and simply nodded.

'I remember when I was about your age, I went out with some mates and we drank whisky in the park. Seemed like a great idea at the time, but when I got up to go home I realised I could barely walk,' he said, chuckling. 'For some reason I was convinced I couldn't chuck up in the street somewhere. God knows why. So I somehow managed to get all the way home. Held onto my stomach that whole way, then opened the door and chucked up in my dad's shoes.'

He looked over at Emily, who was still buried in her phone and not listening to a word he was saying.

'Made me laugh, anyway,' he said. 'More than can be said for my old dad.'

'Yeah,' came the reply from Emily, whose brain had clearly told her she needed to add something to the conversation without actually taking any notice of what had been said.

'I was speaking to Chrissie last night about having dinner together at some point. The three of us,' he said. 'What do you reckon?'

'Yeah, that'd be good.'

'You think? You alright with that?' he asked, still not convinced she was listening to him.

'Yeah, fine.'

'Em? What's up?'

At the sound of her name, she finally looked up, her

eyes slightly bloodshot and clearly tired. 'Nothing. I said it's fine. Just one condition, though.'

'What's that?'

'I get to choose where we go. You'll only choose that shitty Italian dungeon.' She turned back to her phone, her thumbs swiftly tapping away at a text message of some sort.

Jack hoped she wasn't texting a boy. She was at the age where it was unavoidable, he knew, but he was also well aware of the sorts of lads that came from Mildenheath and knew a couple of the circles she'd moved in. He recalled her brief involvement with Ethan Turner, a lad Jack had discovered had a criminal record for violent behaviour, and whose family were well known to the police. He'd had a quiet word with Turner a couple of years ago and made it perfectly clear he wasn't welcome around Emily. Fortunately, it seemed to have worked.

'Nothing wrong with Alessandro's. It wouldn't have lasted forty-odd years otherwise.'

'Yeah, well unfortunately the wallpaper's lasted forty-odd years too. And the carpet.'

'What are your plans for today then?' he asked, keen to change the subject. 'Having a lazy one?'

'Just going to meet some friends. Probably see a film or something.'

'Sounds good. Who're you going with?'

'You wouldn't know them.'

'Not if you don't tell me about them, no.'

'Not sure yet. Depends who can make it. Are you okay with me going out?' she said, looking up at him again.

Jack forced a smile. 'Yeah. Course. No problem at all.'

24

It was a general rule in policing that if you thought things were going alright, the shit was about to hit the fan. There were many things it was unacceptable to say in a police station, and none was more taboo than 'It's a bit quiet today, isn't it?'

Although Jack hadn't said as much, he'd dared to think it, and he was made to regret it the moment the Chief Constable, Charles Hawes, walked into his office.

'Jack, have you got a couple of minutes? The Andrews woman is in and wants to go through a few things.'

Their dislike of Penny Andrews, the county's elected Police and Crime Commissioner, was mutual. Both disliked the idea of PCCs at the best of times, seeing they tended to be career politicians rather than people with any experience of policing. Penny Andrews wasn't even from the local area; she'd spotted a relatively easy seat to win in a relatively conservative area and had coasted to victory at the recent election. The fact that just under fourteen percent of the electorate bothered to turn up to elect her said it all. That this was one of the highest PCC election turnouts in the country said even more about the failed system.

It had always seemed barmy to mix policing and politics, but at least the PCC system didn't try to hide it. Candidates stood on a party ticket, with their party name and logo emblazoned next to their own name on the ballot paper. Jack felt almost certain that Andrews would throw her hat into the ring to be the next Member of Parliament for the local constituency once the longstanding local MP decided he'd had enough.

'If she's on the warpath, it'll take more than a couple of minutes,' Jack said.

Hawes shrugged. 'She's technically my boss.'

'She's technically a cunt.'

'Be polite, Jack.'

'That was polite.'

'I'll give you a minute to grab a coffee and some composure. Meet me up in my office. I'll keep her quiet for a couple of minutes.'

'Good luck with that,' Jack mumbled, watching the Chief Constable leave.

Regardless, he did as he was told and poured himself a quick cup of instant coffee from the machine in the office, wincing at the strong aroma of cat piss as he tried to think only of the caffeine content.

Barely three minutes later, he was in Hawes's office, telling himself he'd play the game and listen to what she had to say. He'd nod and smile and say all the right things, then get back to his real job and forget the woman even existed. That seemed to be the real purpose of Police and Crime Commissioners. A steal at eighty-five grand a year.

'Thank you for joining us, Jack,' Andrews said, declining to use his rank even though the pair weren't altogether acquainted.

'Pleasure, Penny,' Jack replied, catching a glancing scowl from Hawes.

'I just wanted to have a quick chat as, like all residents of the area, I'm concerned about the spate of robberies we've seen recently.'

Jack held back from pointing out she'd only been a resident of the area for a matter of weeks. 'Yes. That's our priority case right now.'

'And I presume it's being treated with all the seriousness that a murder case would?'

'It is a murder case,' Jack replied. 'So yes.'

'Good. And how are you doing for resources? I know the team up at Milton House are more than happy to lend a hand if you're short.'

'We're doing just fine. Making good progress.'

Andrews nodded slowly. 'You don't need to worry about them interfering, you know. We all work together here. They want to catch the people responsible just as much as you do.'

And claim all the credit for it, Jack thought. 'I know. I'm sure they do. But we're making excellent progress, as I say.'

'Charles tells me you had someone in custody. Darren King, was it?'

'Damian. He was released on bail earlier this morning.'

'Do we think he was involved?'

'Not at the moment. His alibi seems to match up. We'll keep digging, though.'

'Anyone else in your crosshairs?'

Jack swallowed. Even though he didn't have any desire to mention PC Theo Curwood, correct procedure would have prevented him from doing so — even to higher ranking officers or the PCC.

He'd put the call in the previous evening before heading home to get changed for his evening out with Chrissie. The whole process had been remarkably odd. They'd listened to the details of what he told them, repeated his statement back to him, then told him they'd take care of it from here and would get back to him in due course. It was now out of his hands, and there was no-one he could talk to about it apart from Wendy, who'd mentioned the concerns to him in the first place.

'One or two,' Jack said. 'Investigations are ongoing. I can't say any more about it at the moment.'

'That's rather convenient, isn't it?' Andrews said.

'Not particularly. Frankly, I'd love to be able to tell you

everything but operational procedures mean you'll just have to trust me.' He stood up and pushed his chair back. 'Now, if you'll excuse me I've got a lot of work on, and we're not getting any closer to catching them while I'm sitting in here chatting about it,' he said, leaving the office before even waiting for a response.

25

Theo Curwood had started to develop a bit of a reputation for community policing, and he didn't mind that one bit. Local business owners had come to rely on him as their point of contact with the police — something which was becoming more necessary every day after the recent spate of armed robberies in and around Mildenheath.

Although the free local crime prevention surveys and advice had been on offer for quite some time, there had been a marked increase in the number of businesses taking the police up on it. It seemed that more and more local business owners were keen to protect themselves from what had happened to Ian Gumbert, not to mention Elsie Fogg.

Local business networks were awash with rumours and scare stories, and the town's Round Table group had recently approached Theo to come and speak to them at their next meeting in an attempt to try to combat the problem head-on. He'd been only too happy to oblige.

That morning he'd been assigned to visit a local independent betting shop, the owner of which had requested the free crime prevention survey. It was easy work, if truth be told. He had colleagues who were out on the front line, getting beaten up and stabbed while trying to keep the public safe, so he really didn't mind knocking around a few shops, telling people to lock their doors and keep an ear out for strange noises.

He'd been thinking of leaving the police for a while now. He'd wanted to be a copper ever since he was a kid, but the job hadn't turned out the way he'd expected. He was just another number on a system, with next to no autonomy and very little of the excitement he craved. Policing wasn't anything like people expected. TV had a lot to answer for.

He went into the shop and greeted the elderly owner, who introduced herself as Pat. She seemed a nice enough lady, but reeked of old carpets. It was almost as if she'd become one with her shop over the decades. The shop had been there for as long as Theo remembered, and probably many years before that.

'I'll be honest with you,' Pat said, grabbing him by the forearm, 'I'm only hanging onto the place out of principle. William Hill offered to buy me out a couple of years back, but I made a promise never to do that. My husband used to run the shop, see. He worked for William Hill many years ago and had a big falling out with them, which is why he set up on his own. That's why the buggers opened two branches on this high street. Trying to squeeze him out. He wouldn't have it. It sort of feels like my duty to do what he would have done and to hold firm, you see what I mean?'

'Absolutely,' Theo replied. 'There aren't enough independent businesses around any more. It's a shame to see them all gobbled up by the big boys.' Although it was worth paying lip service to the woman's views and opinions, Theo knew it was useless. Every local business he went into had a similar story. They were either hanging on for dear life through some sort of family loyalty or a fierce determination to be the captain who goes down with his ship. It was either admirable or foolish; he didn't know which.

The pair spent twenty minutes looking around the shop and the back office. Remarkably, the shop had never been robbed in its history — something almost unheard of for a betting shop. Perhaps it was the case that the big boys were seen as a more justifiable target. After all, they could absorb the losses. They were insured to the hilt. Who'd want to do over a little old lady when there were plenty of huge corporate chains on the same stretch of high street?

The security measures at the shop seemed pretty sound, even for a bookies. The alarm system was fully functioning and linked to the police. The safe was well hidden and of the highest commercial grade available. Bulletproof screens above the counters were, unfortunately, a necessity and were of good quality. The place had clearly been looked after, even if it was in need of a bit of TLC and some new carpets.

'What about CCTV? Is it fully operational?' Theo asked.

'It is, yes.'

'And where does it record and backup onto?'

'It goes onto the computer in the office, love.'

'Can I take a quick look?'

The old lady nodded and led Theo through into the office. She walked over to the desk and jiggled the computer mouse, watching the screen come back to life. She moved the cursor down to the bottom of the screen and clicked on an icon, loading the bank of live CCTV coverage. Theo could see that one or two of the outside cameras were askew, recording far more of the wall than they were of any potentially useful areas.

'Don't worry about those,' Pat said, as if reading his mind. 'We need to get them sorted.'

'Is this computer on all the time?'

'Oh yes. The cameras don't record otherwise.'

Theo nodded. 'And do you do backups?'

'Yes, we've got a man who comes in once a month to do upgrades and things to the computer. Backups, things like that. I don't really understand it, so we pay him on a main-tenance contract and he does that as part of it.'

'So the recordings stay on this machine until he comes

in to back them up elsewhere? They don't get stored anywhere else?'

'No, love. Is that alright?'

Theo smiled and nodded. 'Yes, of course. Absolutely fine.'

26

One of the three covert officers closed the door gently behind him. They'd be in and out within a few minutes. It was yet another way in which things could move very quickly indeed when they had to. He knew nothing of the operation this was a part of, and wasn't aware of whose flat he was in.

He hadn't been told by his superiors that he was there to bug the home of a serving police officer, although it was easy enough to spot whenever that was the case. There'd often be paperwork left lying about, perhaps a staff pass or the telltale shift pattern marked out on the calendar in the kitchen. It was all part of the job. If there were corrupt officers in the force, they needed to be rooted out.

The covert operation had been authorised almost instantly, and was being headed by DCS Andrew Davis. The fact that a woman had died as a direct result of an armed robbery had ensured the decision to investigate on grounds of corruption was made with the utmost speed and diligence. This was a current and live case, and if more lives and livelihoods were potentially at risk, there was no time to lose. There was a very real chance that another robbery could take place either that day or the next. Failure to act in the shortest possible timeframe could reflect very badly on them indeed.

Professional Standards investigations took place entirely independently of the main investigation. DCI Jack Culverhouse and his team would have nothing to do with the investigation into PC Theo Curwood, nor would any other member of the force other than the officer who reported it — plus the Chief Constable — be made aware an investigation was going on. After all, there was no way of knowing how many officers were potentially involved in this corruption, or who they were.

The first part of the operation had been to find a friendly and willing local business owner to assist with the integrity testing side of the investigation. The obvious choice had been the bookmaker's shop run by Pat Dilliard, widow of Paul Dilliard, who'd not only run the shop with his wife for many years before his death, but had also been a prominent local councillor, sitting on the local police authority before authorities were abolished in favour of elected Police and Crime Commissioners in 2012, the same year Paul died. He'd taken his role seriously, and had developed good links with high-ranking local police officers. This made Pat's shop the ideal honeypot for testing Theo Curwood's professional integrity.

She'd been briefed on what to say during the security review. She should intimate that CCTV backups were not done automatically, and only sporadically. They'd also move a couple of the cameras to ensure there were some CCTV dead spots. For PC Curwood's professional integrity to remain intact, these were things he should spot and feed back to Mrs Dilliard, as any competent officer would.

But proving incompetence was not enough. Evidence was needed that PC Curwood was not only failing to high-light security concerns, but that he was using this informa-tion for his own advantage, thus proving corruption. That step would be much harder to prove.

Not only had they begun to trace PC Curwood's phone calls, text messages and emails, but they'd spoken to the Chief Constable to seek authorisation for the usage of covert listening devices in the suspect's flat, at which point he'd been made aware of the investigation into PC Theo Curwood. The Chief Constable had authorised the opera-tion, although realistically he didn't have much choice. A life had already been lost, and denying Professional Stan-dards full access to investigate a matter of potential police corruption would not reflect well on his position.

And so it was that three officers had been sent to PC Theo Curwood's flat. He was known to live alone, and was out at work during the time of the bugging operation, but the lead officer had been instructed to knock at the door — just in case. If someone were to answer, he'd say he was from a neighbouring block and wondered if anyone had seen a small black cat, which had gone missing a day or two previous. It was simple and innocent enough.

Fortunately, no-one had answered, and he'd let himself in by picking the lock on the door. The flat wasn't alarmed, but that didn't matter either — there were numerous ways of getting around those if they needed to.

The covert listening devices used GSM technology — the same gadgetry that enabled mobile phones to work without wires. They were not much bigger than the SIM card they contained, although they were extremely powerful in a policing sense.

Having scoured the living room for the best available position, he bent down in the corner and unscrewed the face plate from the double wall socket. It was a dangerous job — they couldn't risk switching off the power at the fuse board and alerting the suspect to their earlier presence by means of his household electronics having reset themselves. If done properly, though, he wouldn't need to make contact with any live wires. The covert listening device would simply slot inside the back of the existing facia, clip onto the correct wire for a constant power source and continually transmit audio via the SIM card installed within in.

Once he'd installed the device and screwed the face plate back onto the wall, he took his mobile phone out of his pocket and dialled the number of the SIM. The call connected immediately, and he tapped the face plate lightly with his screwdriver, hearing the loud boom broadcast through his phone as the ultra sensitive microphone demonstrated its capabilities.

Next, he moved into the bedroom, then the kitchen and did the same with a socket in each of those rooms. The whole operation took less than five minutes. It would have been quicker if they'd had three officers inside, but they knew they had plenty of time.

When he was done he left the flat, locking the door behind him again. Without saying a word to his colleague who'd been waiting on the stairwell as a lookout, they jogged back down the stairs, rejoining their third colleague in the downstairs lobby before making their way back to the car.

27

When Jack Culverhouse had a bee in his bonnet, there was very little anyone else could do.

He was understandably frustrated that Professional Standards had taken over the investigation into PC Theo Curwood — as was their remit and entire reason for existence — and was clearly struggling with the loss of control in that area.

'I don't know what they think they're going to be able to do that I can't,' he'd told Wendy earlier that morning in his office. 'The whole unit's full of wet university graduates and computer analysts. That'll never beat looking some scrote dead in the eyes and seeing him shit himself right in front of you. You can't beat intuition and experience when it comes to spotting a fucking liar, Knight.'

Wendy had, like most people who'd worked with Jack Culverhouse, known that he was a fan of the old school methods of policing, but it was rare that he went off on a rant quite like this one.

It was clear to her that he was going to become a liability, but at the same time he had an unbeatable record for successful investigations when his head was in the right place.

So far she'd managed to stop him from approaching PC Curwood and interrogating him himself, but it was only a matter of time before something knocked him over the edge and he got to the point where nothing would stand in his way. That was why she'd reluctantly kept her mouth shut when he said he was going to visit Sophie McAreavey, part-time employee at Fogg's jewellers.

'I only worked there a few hours a week. On a casual basis, like,' she said, sitting on the sofa in her parents' living room while her mother and father hovered behind her.

Wendy had accompanied Jack to Sophie's house, keen to provide a calming presence should he decide to explode under the pressure.

'And you were there on the day the police came to do the security review?' Jack asked.

'Yeah. Elsie normally asked me to come in whenever she had to do something, like bank meetings, visiting family, all that sort of thing. Sometimes if it was going to be busy, like in the run up to Christmas or Mother's Day, I'd do a few days in the week too. But she knew she had this meeting with the police, so she asked me to come in and cover while she was busy doing that.'

'And did Elsie mention what was said during the meeting?'

'She didn't need to. That place is tiny. You can hear everything.'

'Do you remember the recommendations he made?'

'Well, he told her she needed a new back door, but that wasn't exactly a surprise. I'd been telling her that myself. I've seen better doors on garden sheds.'

'This is the door at the back of the premises, leading through the office?'

'Yeah, that one. He said the bolts could be ripped off pretty easily and they'd be able to smash through the door with an axe if they wanted to. It was only cheap wood, like.'

Sophie's father took half a step forward, making the sort of nervous stuttering sound some people made when they were trying to make it clear they wanted to talk.

'Do you mind if I ask what this is all about?' he said.

'It's just routine,' Wendy replied, before Jack could speak. 'Because the shop was subsequently robbed, we need to make sure the advice we gave was sound. It helps us spot any weak points in the crime prevention strategy and to enable us to improve the advice we give in the future.'

Sophie's father seemed satisfied with this, and took half a step back again.

'Did the officer give a list of companies that Mrs Fogg could get a more secure door from?' Jack asked.

'Yeah, he did, but I dunno if I remember the name. I've

seen their vans about town and that, but I can't remember what it's called. "Super" or something like that, I think.'

'Supreme Locks and Glazing?'

'Yeah, that's the one. Supreme. Like the chicken.'

'And what about the others?'

'What others?' Sophie asked.

'Was there not a list of approved companies?'

'Nah, that was the only one. He said that was the only one the police recommended.'

Wendy looked at Jack. She could see in his eyes that something dark was brewing.

28

Jack marched down the McAreaveys' front path and back
to his car like a man possessed. As Wendy got into the
passenger seat, Jack thumped the steering wheel with both
hands.

'Knew it. I fucking knew it. The cunt's in league with
McCann. There's you lot telling me it's all a big coincidence and that I've got some sort of vendetta against him,
and I was right all along. We've got a fucking bent copper
telling people Gary McCann's the only person who can
keep their business secure. Like telling a turkey Bernard
Matthews wants to give them a cuddle.'

Wendy wanted to tell him there could be other possibil-
ities. She would have loved to have suggested that maybe
Theo had a brother or a friend who worked for Supreme
Locks and Glazing, that perhaps he'd forgotten the list of
companies and that was the only one he could remember.

But she couldn't. Coincidences didn't convince judges or juries, but it was fair to say they often convinced detectives.

She sat in silence for a moment or two as Jack tried to calm himself down.

'Right,' he said, eventually. 'We're going to Peal End.'

'What? Why?'

'Because we need to speak to Ian Gumbert. We need to see if he got the same shitty advice as Elsie Fogg. At least he's still alive to tell us.'

Before Wendy could protest, Jack had swung the car back out onto the main road and was heading in the direction of the village of Peal End.

When they got there, he marched up the driveway towards the front door and banged on it four times with his fist. Wendy supposed it would help vent more frustration than simply pressing the doorbell.

Ian Gumbert seemed surprised to see them, but also appeared to recognise them, and welcome them into the house.

'Bringing good news, I hope. Have you caught them?'

'Not quite,' Jack replied, through gritted teeth. 'Although I feel we're getting closer all the time. We were hoping you might be able to help us with that, actually.'

'Oh? How so?'

'Do you happen to remember if the officer who carried out the crime prevention survey on your premises recommended a particular list of companies you might want to use to improve your security?'

'I don't think he gave a list, no. He did mention one camera company, but I told him I was happy with the dummy ones.'

'Even though he advised you a proper CCTV system would be far better for your security?'

'And far worse for my profit margins.'

'I'd bet you your bottom dollar — if you had one left — that it would have cost you a hell of a lot less than the forty-five grand you lost on the night of the robberies.'

Gumbert shuffled awkwardly. 'Well, it's all academic now. I've hired a private security firm to help avoid any more little... mishaps.'

Jack raised an eyebrow. 'Private security firm?'

'Yep.'

'How'd you find them?'

'I didn't. They came to me after the robberies. PC Curwood recommended them.'

29

The crisp chill in the evening air was lost on Theo Curwood thanks to the four pints he'd enjoyed at the Spit-fire on his way home that evening. He'd left his car in the pub's car park, which doubled as the car park for the parade of shops next to it, and was walking the last few hundred yards home. He could never get parked anywhere near his flat as it was, and it allowed him to enjoy a couple of drinks after work before hitting the sack. He had tomorrow off, so he'd pick the car up in the morning if there was a space outside the flat once his neighbours had gone to work.

He was starting to wonder when the streetlights were going to be fixed along this stretch of Heathcote Road. They'd been out for at least a week now. He wasn't the sort of person who tended to worry about the dark, but he was starting to become much more edgy in general recently, and things like this weren't helping him. Not one bit.

He glanced furtively over his shoulder, sure someone was watching or following him, but he could see no-one. *You're just being paranoid*, he told himself. *If you carry on like this, people are going to realise something's up.*

Before he even realised what he was doing, he ducked down the alleyway to his left, marching as quickly as he could, before stepping into a gap by a garage block and standing with his back against it.

He needed to compose himself. This wasn't the way things got done.

They'd told him they'd look after him, but the truth was he hadn't heard from them in a day or two. He'd gone into the Spitfire hoping he might be able to update someone — or that someone might update him — but it had been full of old boys talking about their medication and how the old butcher's shop on the corner used to be miles better than the supermarket that sprung up in town and finished it off.

He felt he was getting in further over his head than he'd ever intended to. Events hadn't quite gone to plan, but that meant there was no backing out now. Not now a woman was dead. His only option now was to see this out and and wait for it all to blow over. As much as he might have wanted it, there was no going back.

He knew how much money the bookies took, and that would definitely provide a pretty lucrative payday. Then again, he'd thought that about the petrol stations, but they still hadn't been happy — even with forty-five grand. They wanted more. But there wasn't more. At least not amongst the newsagents, coffee shops and tanning studios that lined the high street. But the bookies might just be his way out.

There was no way he could tell them he'd had enough. He knew that. All they needed to do was make a phone call and he'd be thrown under the bus. They had more than enough on him, and it was no longer a case of robbery. He'd be an accessory to murder.

Content enough that the coast was clear, he stepped back out into the alleyway and returned to Heathcote Road. He headed straight home, but a little quicker this time.

When he got back to his flat, he darted up the stairs, unlocked his front door and closed it behind him, making sure he locked the latch, deadbolt and security chain. He could already feel his heart rate returning to normal.

Without turning on the lights, he stepped into his living room and peered round the edge of the curtains, down onto the street below. He couldn't see anything, but then he didn't know what he was looking for.

He went into his bedroom, knelt down on the floor beside his bed and pulled the shoebox out from under it.

He paused for a moment, unsure whether or not this was the right thing to do. Cosy chats in the corner of the pub were far more secure and far less risky, but what choice did he have? He hadn't heard anything from them, and that worried him. In any case, he had something to pass on to them. Something which might give him some leverage or bargaining power in convincing them to leave him be.

He took the lid off the shoebox and rummaged around inside the shredded paper before pulling out a cheap, basic mobile phone.

They'd given him the burner when he'd agreed to help out and pass information on to them, and he'd only switched it on once since then. Everything else had been done through the pub. He should only use it in emergencies, they told him. Well, fuck, this was an emergency. A woman was dead, they'd gone quiet and he was starting to get the jitters. All police officers knew what came next when someone got the jitters. That was when things started to fall apart. That was when friends and family noticed a change in behaviour and made a casual remark to a police officer. It was when deviations from normal patterns were spotted. It was the beginning of the end.

Theo couldn't risk that happening. So yes, this was an emergency.

He held down the button on the top of the phone and watched as the screen lit up, flooding the small room with white light.

He stood and walked into his living room as he called one of the pre-programmed numbers and waited for it to connect.

'Hello? Yeah, it's me. Listen, I've not seen you around for a couple of days so I wanted to give you an update. I think I've got another one for you. Bookies in town. You around tomorrow?'

The person at the other end said nothing, then terminated the call.

Theo stood for a moment, wondering if perhaps there'd been some sort of fault on the line, but deep down he knew that wasn't the case. This was all part of it. They were keeping him at arm's length, hedging their bets. He'd go to the Spitfire tomorrow in any case, and see if anyone was around. If they weren't there then, they could go fuck themselves. He was done.

He'd wanted out for a long time. Out of this, out of the job, out of his shitty meaningless existence. He'd always regretted not taking some time between school and work to go travelling, see some of the world. He'd always fancied Asia and the Far East. Maybe he'd use this as an opportunity to grasp it with both hands.

He bent over to pick up his laptop, the compression forcing out a belch which allowed him to taste the remnants of those four pints. He put the laptop on the coffee table in front of him, sat down on the sofa and loaded up his web browser.

He typed 'flights to Japan' in the search bar and browsed the results, hoping for something leaving Heathrow within the next couple of days. Fuck the job — he'd go AWOL. What was the worst they could do?

Maybe he'd call in sick, tell them he was suffering from depression or something. He'd had a couple of colleagues who'd had time off with depression, and the force did absolutely nothing. No support, no follow-up phone calls, no checks on his welfare. That sounded absolutely ideal right now.

He needed another drink. He cleared his throat and stood up before going to cross the hallway into his kitchen. As he did so, he stopped and looked towards the front door.

The entry mat had moved. He was sure of it.

He was always so careful to make sure it sat square against the doorframe, every time he went in or out. There was no way he'd have left it skew-whiff like that. He'd only had four pints.

Before he could process what was happening, he saw a brief blur, then felt the crushing pain of a large forearm tightening around his neck.

30

Jack had waited to feed the extra information about Theo Curwood back to Professional Standards. When he and Wendy got back the previous afternoon, he'd gone into his office on the pretext of making the call, but decided against it. This was something he needed to sleep on. In any case, he couldn't risk having to tell Professional Standards he'd been conducting his own investigation into Curwood. That was well beyond his remit, and would likely result in Jack being the next subject of their investigation.

The first knock on his office door that morning was from Wendy.

'Want a coffee?' she asked.

She never asked him if he wanted coffee. Everyone got their own. That was the way it was.

'No thanks,' he replied, not looking up from the stack of papers in front of him.

'How are you feeling?' she eventually asked.

'Fucked off.'

Wendy stepped forward and sat down in the chair in front of his desk. 'Look, it happens. It's not your fault. It's not anyone's fault but his.'

Jack shook his head. 'We rooted all this shit out years ago. Nowadays there's no such thing as a corrupt officer. Only officers who've been corrupted.'

'You still think McCann's behind this?' she asked.

'I *know* McCann is behind this.'

Wendy raised her eyebrows briefly.

'What? You don't think he is?' Jack said.

'I don't know. All signs seem to point that way, but how many times have we been in that situation? He's the master of covering his own arse. Proving anything and nailing him to something is going to be impossible.'

'He's a bloody director of the company that fitted the door to Elsie Fogg's shop. And the security company Gumbert's hired to look after his petrol stations.'

This was news to Wendy. 'Seriously?'

'Seriously.'

'But that makes no sense. Why would McCann want to be involved with the security at the petrol stations *after* he's rinsed them for forty-five grand? Doesn't seem sensible to return to the scene of the crime. And in any case, Gumbert's likely to be ruined by losing all that money. The petrol stations probably won't be there in a few months.'

Jack scrunched his eyes and rubbed the bridge of his

nose. 'Trust me, I've been lying awake all night thinking about that. The best I can come up with is that this is another way of him getting his foot in the door ready to "rescue" another failing business. I'd bet my house on him being listed as a director within weeks.'

'Wouldn't that be massively risky, though? Especially for him. He's not the sort of person to take those risks. He always makes sure he's got himself covered.'

'That's the problem. That's why it doesn't make any sense. But I had another thought. What if one of the side benefits of these robberies is that McCann's company can frighten local business owners into feeling they need extra security, which he then steps in and provides? It's something that happens all the time in the big cities. It's like a silent, unspoken, covert protection racket.'

'It's possible,' Wendy said. 'But again, risky.'

'All crime involves some sort of risk. And you and I both know he's as criminal as it gets.'

'And Theo's his information man?'

'Makes sense. He lives up the end of Heathcote Road. Would make sense that his local is the Spitfire. And we both know who owns that.'

'McCann.'

'The one and only. Wouldn't surprise me one bit if he found out Theo was a copper and somehow managed to threaten or scare him into passing on information about the security setups in local businesses.'

'Again, possible. Or maybe Theo's just a bad egg. It does happen.'

Jack shook his head. 'No. Not like that, it doesn't. Not when McCann's around. If anything, Theo needs our help. We need to get him back onside. We need to give him support and protection and find out what really happened. That way we can nail that cunt McCann once and for all. Come on,' he said, standing up. 'Grab your coat.'

'Why? Where are we going?'

'Theo's got the day off. I checked. We're going to pay him a little visit.'

31

'Look, let's not be too hasty, shall we?' Wendy said. 'We can't go treading on the toes of Professional Standards.'

'Why not?'

'Because Theo is their investigation. Our job is to find out who's responsible for the robberies and the death of Elsie Fogg.'

'And what if it's the same person? We know it is. There's nothing saying we can't speak to someone we suspect of being involved in a major crime we're investigating.'

'I'm not sure that's true now Professional Standards are involved,' Wendy replied.

Jack pushed his tongue into the inside of his cheek and rolled his jaw. 'Fuck it. I'm doing it anyway,' he said.

'Wait. Think about it for a second. It's not even Professional Standards we want to worry about. Yeah, alright, you'd probably be able to argue your case with them and we'd be in the clear, but having you referred to Professional Standards isn't going to go down well with Penny Andrews, is it? She'll have your guts for garters.'

Jack seemed to consider this for a moment. 'To be honest with you, I couldn't give a shit what that woman thinks.'

'Nor me,' Wendy said. 'But she's the decision maker. Do you really want to give her more ammunition to shut us down and move everything to Milton House?'

'We can't just let this go, Knight. We're onto something here. Something big. I can taste it.'

'I know. I'm not suggesting we let it go. I'm just saying there might be better ways of doing things.'

'Like what?'

Wendy hadn't thought that far ahead. 'Why don't we try phoning him first?' she said.

'What, and spooking the fucker so he does a runner?'

'No, we tread a bit more carefully than that.'

'How? We can't just ring him up and ask him if he's being leant on by Gary McCann. He'll peg it.'

'And how is going round to his house and asking the same thing going to be any different?'

'He can't do a runner if we're there.'

Wendy chuckled to herself. 'With all due respect, I think he'd stand a pretty good chance. Neither of us is in shape.'

'Oi. Round is a shape.'

'Look, just let me phone him first,' Wendy said. 'I'll think of something. The most important thing right now is not spooking Theo or getting ourselves on the wrong side of Professional Standards. Can I use your computer?' she said, gesturing towards his desk.

'Might as well. I can't make head nor tail of the bloody thing.'

Wendy took a few moments to navigate her way through the awkward and clunky Mildenheath Police intranet system, eventually finding Theo Curwood's mobile phone number in the staff directory.

She typed the number into her own mobile, then pressed *Call*.

The phone took a couple of seconds to dial, then began to ring. After a while, it became clear Theo wasn't going to answer.

'I don't think he's going to pick up,' Wendy said, turning round to look at Jack.

But he was gone.

Wendy eventually caught up with Jack in the car park.

'Guv! Wait!'

'Get your arse in the car within the next five seconds and you can come,' he yelled back across the tarmac.

Wendy jogged over to the car and got in. 'I thought we agreed we were ringing him first?' she said, out of breath.

'We did ring him first. He didn't answer. Ten quid says

he's seen the call come in, panicked and legged it. Just like I said he would. That's why,' he said, his wheels screeching on the ground as he accelerated out of the car park and onto the main road, 'we're not hanging around.'

It took them just over four minutes to reach Theo Curwood's flat. It would usually have taken longer, but Jack wasn't hanging around. Wendy wondered if his car's suspension felt as sore as her spine after having hit each speed bump on the way at over forty miles an hour.

They pulled up in a space right outside the block of flats and went inside. When they reached the front door of Theo's flat, Jack held his finger down on the buzzer for a good five seconds, before taking it off and knocking — just to make it perfectly clear there was someone at the door.

After a short while, it became clear there was no answer.

'He's either out somewhere, driving or has done a bunk,' Wendy said.

'In which case, we need to go after him,' Jack replied.

'Go where? He could have gone anywhere, any time. And in any case, it's not our problem. PS are investigating him. If they're doing their job properly, they'll be tracking him.'

'Yeah. *If.*'

Wendy watched as Jack stepped back away from the door, defeated in his chase. 'Let's just head back, yeah? We can update PS and let them know we wanted to speak to Theo about something else, but that we couldn't get hold of hi—'

Wendy's sentence was interrupted by the sound of the bottom of Jack's boot smashing into the locking mechanism of Theo's front door, sending it swinging back against the wall with a crash.

'Honey, we're home!' he called into the flat as he marched inside.

Wendy let out a groan of frustration as she followed him, watching as he made his way down the corridor, pushing open the bedroom and bathroom doors to his left and right, peering inside.

Jack got to the end of the corridor and pushed open the door to his right — the kitchen — before turning and looking in the opposite direction, into the living room.

Wendy could tell immediately that something was very wrong. 'What is it?' she asked.

She stepped forward so she could see into the room too. See what Jack was looking at. Theo Curwood was hanging from the light fitting, a crude noose tied around his neck.

It was clear why Jack had stayed on the spot and not made any attempt to get him down: Theo was grey, his face swollen. He was a long time dead.

32

The atmosphere in the incident room the next day was different from anything they'd felt in a long time. It was always shocking when a police officer died, whether in the line of duty or through other means, but for Jack and Wendy the shock was even more acute.

Whereas the rest of their colleagues believed this to be a tragic moment, they knew otherwise. They were aware of Theo Curwood's involvement with the robberies and the death of Elsie Fogg. He hadn't just been a police officer who'd died — this was the result of a level of dark corruption which would have far-reaching and dramatic repercussions.

Jack and Wendy, having been unable to listen to any more of the talk about how Theo was a much-loved colleague and his death was so tragic, had decamped to

Jack's office, where they could at least speak to each other in a frank and honest manner.

'Bit fucking convenient, if you ask me,' Jack said, leaning back in his chair, his arms folded across his chest.

'Taking the easy way out, you mean?'

Jack shook his head. 'Quite the opposite. There's no way it was suicide.'

'We don't know yet. Not until the coroner's report. But there wasn't anyone at the scene who thought it was anything else. From what I hear, no concerns have been raised.'

'I'm not having it. There's more to it than this.'

'Think about it, though,' Wendy said. 'It fits the pattern you mentioned yesterday. If Theo was just a young, naive officer who managed to have his arm twisted by McCann — or somebody — into providing information in return for some quick cash, there's every chance he would've panicked when Elsie Fogg died. Maybe the gang put pressure on him to keep quiet, get more information, who knows? Things will have stepped up a gear, massively. You reckoned he was going to leg it. Maybe you weren't so far from the truth.'

Jack seemed to think about this for a moment, before shaking his head again, biting his lip.

'Nah, I'm not buying it. Theo had answers. We know he did. When Elsie Fogg ended up dead, McCann and his gang knew they had to tidy up. They knew there was someone outside their circle, someone inside ours, who knew what had happened. Knew who was involved. There's a reason CSI found nothing in his flat. If Theo Curwood was so heavily involved in all this to the point he'd left his name all over the reports, there'd be some sorts of traces in his own fucking flat. Something doesn't sit right here, Knight. And don't even think about giving me a bollocking about following the facts instead of my instincts.'

Wendy raised her hands in mock surrender. 'I wasn't going to.'

'Good.'

The atmosphere was pierced by a knocking at the door.

'Come in,' Culverhouse growled.

The pair could see Debbie Weston looked visibly distressed.

'Guv, I hate to do this to you, but I'm really not doing too well today.'

'In what way?'

'The news this morning. It's kind of... hit me. Hard.'

Culverhouse narrowed his eyes. 'Why? Did you know him?'

'Well, no. No, of course not. But it still gets to you, doesn't it? Thin blue line getting even thinner, and all that.'

'Are you telling me you want to piss off home again? You've barely been back five minutes.'

'I think I'd be far more use to you tomorrow if I have the rest of the day to get my head straight, yes.'

'Sometimes I think you'd be far more use as a fucking hatstand, but there we go. Go on. Piss off then.'

'I think you're being a bit harsh on her,' Wendy said once Debbie had left the office.'

'It's a good job I didn't ask what you think, then.'

'She's been having a tough time of it recently. We've all got a duty to look after each other.'

'No, we've got a duty to catch the bastards who've been ruining — and ending — people's lives. That's the only thing I care about. Speaking of which. I'm going to get Steve and Frank to do some door-to-door enquiries, see if we can find out if anyone saw someone going in or out of Theo's flat yesterday or the day before. You and Ryan can get onto finding CCTV. There'll be some at the flats, I'm sure of it. Contact the freeholder and the residents' association and find out who's in control of it.'

'Whoa, hang on a second,' Wendy said, her voice firm. 'We can't do any of that. That's a Professional Standards investigation. We can't touch it.'

'No it's not. Professional Standards were looking into Theo. He's dead. The only person who'll be looking into him is the pathologist.'

'But if there's wider-reaching corruption, that's PS's job. Not ours.'

Jack looked at her for a moment. 'What do you mean wider-reaching corruption?'

'What I mean is they need to determine whether or not it ended with Theo. They need to find out how he built those links, what information was passed back and how. And whether there are other links.'

Jack leaned forward, narrowing his eyes. 'Are you trying to make out there are other coppers in McCann's pocket?'

'I'm just saying we can't be too careful.'

'Yes we fucking can. We spend our entire lives being too careful. That's how bastards get away with stuff.'

'I just think we should keep this between ourselves and Professional Standards. Neither of us would've thought in a million years Theo Curwood was corrupt. What's to say we aren't in for another surprise? We really need to be careful. We can't go repeating what we know to anyone else.'

Jack Culverhouse's face suddenly turned very dark. 'You think we've got one on the team, don't you,' he said, more as a statement than a question.'

'No! No, of course not. But they might repeat something to someone else, or leave some sort of trail with phone calls which tips another person off. Everything has to be kept tight. You know the procedure.'

'My team are not corrupt.'

'I know that.'

'They've all worked with me for years. I know them better than their own fucking wives. I bet I've seen Steve's cock in the bogs more time than his missus has, that's for sure. Theo Curwood was a one-off. He was young and stupid. He had his head turned by money. It happens. He was the victim, not the culprit. McCann is the one we want. And I'm telling you now, it ends with him.'

Wendy knew it was best not to argue. Instead, she forced a smile and nodded.

33

Jack felt blessed to have some light relief that evening, in the form of the planned meal with Chrissie and Emily. They'd finally settled on an American-style diner three miles outside Mildenheath, at Emily's request. His daughter had told him she'd get a friend to drop her off on the way back from the cinema, but — an hour after they'd arranged to meet — she still wasn't there.

'I'm so sorry about this,' he said to Chrissie. 'She's a bloody nightmare sometimes.'

'Still not answering her phone?'

'Nope. Straight through to voicemail. She does this sometimes. I'm sorry. I don't know what to say.'

'You don't need to say anything. We're having fun as it is. We can wait.'

Jack looked down at the plate of nachos in front of him, growing soggier by the second under the weight of salsa, guacamole and luminous orange cheese. He wasn't a fan of American food at the best of times, and really didn't see the point in paying to come out and eat a massive bowl of crisps — especially when someone had dumped the contents of a few Heinz jars on top of them.

'Maybe it's just a bit of a weird situation for her,' Chrissie said.

Jack shook his head. 'She told me it wasn't. She said it sounded like a great idea, as long as she could choose where we ate.'

'Well she's obviously keen on the place, then. I can't see her bailing at the last minute.'

'I'm just so sorry.'

'Honestly,' Chrissie said, leaning across the table and placing her hand on Jack's wrist. 'Don't be. There's no need.'

Within a few minutes, the conversation had started to flow properly, with the acceptance that Emily wasn't going to turn up.

'Do you still see any of those colleagues?' Jack asked, eliciting a small chuckle from Chrissie. 'What? What did I say?'

'Nothing. I just knew that'd been on your mind ever since I mentioned it.'

'Only asking. I just wondered if you were doing the modern thing and seeing multiple people at the same time. Hedging your bets, or whatever it is.'

Chrissie smiled. 'No. Only you.'

'Good. Same here.'

'Well that much was obvious,' she replied, laughing.

Jack took his phone out of his pocket and checked the screen again. Still no texts from Emily. He looked up to see Chrissie's mind had clearly moved on to something else. 'What's up?' he asked.

'Nothing.'

'No, come on. I can see something is.'

'Look, it's not for me to intrude on the father-daughter relationship, and this probably isn't the place to bring it up, but I've just had a couple of concerns recently, that's all.'

'About Emily?'

'Yeah.'

'But you said earlier it wasn't a problem.'

'It isn't. We're still having fun. But what I mean is, it's not entirely out of character for her at the moment.'

Jack leaned forward. 'What do you mean?'

Chrissie let out a small sigh. 'She's been late to school quite a bit recently. She's seemed sort of... distant. I mean, she's never been the highest-achieving pupil, even though she's clearly a smart cookie, but she tried to pay attention. Over the last week or two she's sort of drifted a bit. Doesn't seem quite with it.'

Jack's heart lurched a little. He thought back to Emily's hangover the other morning, having vomited in the bathroom. What if it wasn't alcohol? What if she'd been experimenting with harder drugs?

Would he have spotted the change in her? Had he been

perceptive enough? He supposed school teachers were trained to look out for these small, subtle changes, especially in kids Emily's age. All of a sudden, something seemed very wrong. The mood changes, the unreliability. It all started to make sense.

'Look, I'm sorry. I need to get back home. I'm spending too much time worrying. I need to see if she's there.'

'It's fine,' Chrissie said. 'I understand.'

Jack smiled at her. She was always so calm and collected. He felt terrible letting her down.

'I just need to check she's alright.'

'I get it. Don't worry. You go.'

Jack took a twenty-pound note out of his wallet and put it on the table, before leaning over and giving Chrissie a kiss on the cheek.

'That's for the soggy crisps, by the way.'

'The twenty-pound note or the kiss?'

'Both.'

By the time he got home, his worry had turned to fury. How could Emily get involved with people like that? He realised her home life had been far from conventional, but she knew better than to get mixed up with drugs.

When he got in, he found Emily sitting on the sofa, watching a film.

'What's going on, Em?' he said, talking to the back of her head.

'I dunno, I came in halfway through.'

'You know damn well what I mean. Why didn't you meet us at the restaurant? It was your idea.'

'No, it was your idea. I just said I'd prefer to eat there than that shitty Italian place.'

'So why not turn up?' he asked, choosing to ignore the slight slur in her voice. He thought he'd also spotted a light sniffle, too. He hoped it wasn't a sign of cocaine use.

'Couldn't get a lift.'

'Did you not think to ring me or text me to let me know? We waited over an hour for you.'

'Sorry. I turned my phone off in the cinema and forgot to turn it back on.'

'But you knew you were meant to be meeting us, Em! We had it all arranged. You knew the place, you knew the time. Surely when you realised you couldn't make it you would've switched your phone on and called me or texted me?'

Emily's voice was weak. 'I said sorry.'

Jack stepped forward to look at her, and in that moment he realised she was crying, but trying her hardest to make it look as if she wasn't.

'Em, what's wrong? Talk to me.'

Emily stood up and darted towards the stairs. 'Fuck off. Just fuck off, okay?'

He watched as his daughter ran up the stairs to her bedroom, wincing as the door slammed and the house shook.

34

If he wasn't capable of doing much else as a father, he was sure as hell going to make sure he could rustle up Emily a decent cooked breakfast. He'd begun to notice things about her now — things he'd been blind to — like the fact she'd clearly lost some weight recently.

He watched the bacon sizzling in the pan, wondering if he should chuck in another knob of butter to add a few extra calories.

'Where'd you get that from?' Emily asked — more or less the first words she'd said to her dad all morning.

'Supermarket. Why?'

'It smells weird.'

Jack hovered his nose over the pan. 'Seems fine to me.' His attention was taken away by a text message pinging through on his phone. He picked it up and saw it was from Chrissie. He couldn't read the full message without unlocking the screen, but could see the first few words and that she was apologising for the previous evening. He didn't need her apologies. 'How's everything going at school?' he asked Emily, serving up the food.

'Fine.'

'Getting on alright with everyone?'

'Yeah fine.'

He put her plate down on the table in front of her — a gesture which was greeted by Emily staring at it.

'What's wrong?'

'The egg's runny.'

'I know,' he said. 'You love runny eggs.'

'I used to.'

'Alright, well give it here. I'll pop it back in the pan.'

'No, don't worry. I'll just leave it.'

Jack thought about arguing back, but decided against it. It rarely did any good to argue with Emily, especially when she was in one of these moods.

'What have you got today, then?' he asked her, having eaten most of their meal in silence.

'Dunno, not checked. History I think.'

'Do you enjoy it?'

'Spose.'

'Used to be one of my favourite subjects, that.'

'What, back when they called it Current Affairs?'

For the first time that morning, Jack smiled. 'Yeah. Something like that. Listen, do you want a lift in today? I'm on a late start and I've got to run a couple of errands before I go into the office, so it'll save you getting the bus.'

'Nah, it's cool. I quite like the bus journey.'

'Alright. Suit yourself,' Jack said. The last time he'd had to get on a local bus he'd got off certain he needed a double hip replacement.

A minute or so later, Emily got up from the table without saying anything and went back upstairs.

Something wasn't right. Something definitely wasn't right. And he needed answers.

He pottered about the house while he waited for Emily to get dressed for school, making a show of cleaning things that didn't really need cleaning. Twenty minutes later, she came downstairs and shouted a passing goodbye as she let herself out and closed the door behind her. Jack watched as she walked up the driveway to the road and turned left towards the bus stop. In that moment, he felt a sudden pang of urgency and his instincts kicked in. He grabbed his coat and keys, put on a pair of shoes and closed the front door behind him, pulling his coat closed against the cold.

He walked up to the end of the driveway and peered around the conifers, waiting for Emily to round the corner at the end of the road. Once she had, he walked quickly after her until he'd reached the end of the street himself. From there, he could see across the low-walled front gardens to the bus stop from which Emily caught the bus to school. He could see Emily, but she was standing at the bus stop on the other side of the road.

Jack knew any buses stopping there would be going in the opposite direction from the school. He waited for a minute or so, unsure what to do next. He couldn't approach her, or he'd end up pushing her away. All he could do was watch.

As he realised that, he was jolted to alertness by the sound of a loud diesel bus roaring past him and coming to a stop further down the road, right next to where Emily was waiting.

He peered carefully through the dusty windows and from that distance could just about make out Emily getting onto the bus. In any other situation, Emily's behaviour could hardly be considered out of character.

But it wasn't her getting on the wrong bus and heading away from the school that concerned Jack. It was what was showing on the destination sign.

35

Jack jogged back up the road towards the house and went inside to grab his car keys.

He knew the rough route the bus took, and he also knew he could get to the destination quicker than it could — and on a parallel route which would mean Emily wouldn't spot his car.

He unlocked the car and got in, started up the engine and pulled out onto the street.

A million thoughts were racing through his mind. There was always the possibility that her destination wasn't the same as that of the bus — that she could conceivably get off at any stop along the way — but Jack had a horrible sinking feeling in the pit of his stomach which told him that was not the case. Intuition rarely let him down.

Almost ten minutes later, he'd arrived. He pulled over at the side of the road a little further down, and waited for the bus to round the corner. He pulled his phone out of his pocket and Googled the timetable. The bus was due to arrive in less than two minutes.

Jack had taken a slightly quicker and more direct route, but they would have made up some lost time in the bus lanes along the main road. With only two minutes to spare, there can barely have been another stop or two between Jack's house and here. That made him even surer that the bus's destination was to be Emily's, too.

He watched a bus enter the drop-off point. It was green and had come from the opposite direction, but this was clearly where the local buses did their drop-offs.

He thought of all the reasons why Emily might be coming here. Some of them were entirely innocent, but his brain automatically focused on those which were not.

He realised he'd been daydreaming and hadn't been watching the time. Before he could glance at the clock, he registered a red bus rounding the corner and indicating into the bus drop-off area. He could see Emily on board, her head leaning against the window, her long hair mopping up condensation as the bus lulled and bounced over the threshold to its destination.

Jack climbed out of the car to get a better view, and watched as Emily got off the bus and embraced Ethan Turner.

He could feel the anger rising inside him as he watched this. Ethan was a criminal from a family of criminals, and Jack had warned him a couple of years ago — in no uncertain terms — that he was not to contact Emily or set foot within a hundred yards of her. It took every ounce of willpower not to walk straight over and punch him square in the face.

But it wasn't just willpower that was stopping him. It was the realisation of what was happening. It was a series of jigsaw pieces falling into place, revealing the whole picture. How could he have been so stupid? Why didn't he see it earlier?

He watched as Emily and Ethan, hand in hand, entered Mildenheath Hospital's maternity wing.

36

Jack arrived at the station with a smorgasbord of emotions running through him. Anger. Fury. Disappointment. Fear. Elation. Despair.

As far as he'd been aware, Ethan Turner was off the scene. When had he come back? When had she been seeing him? And for how long had she been pregnant?

He'd always been a man who was in control, but now he felt as if he was losing his grip on everything. The investigation at work was running away from him, he was on the verge of losing his autonomy to the desk jockeys at Milton House and now this.

He'd never been in control of Emily. No-one had. And he wouldn't have wanted to be. But he had at least laboured under the misapprehension that she would have felt comfortable telling him something like this. As far as she knew, Jack had no problem with Ethan. He'd comforted her and supported her when the lad had told her he didn't want to see her any more. She had no reason not to come to him now.

Unless.

Unless Ethan Turner had got back in touch with Emily and told her exactly what Jack had done to him. The threats he'd made. The way Jack had pinned him up against a wall and given him no option.

Jack pushed those thoughts from his mind. Emily was too much like her mother to have let that lie. She couldn't have kept that knowledge to herself. She would have confronted her dad within seconds. That just left the horrifying, gut-wrenching realisation that she hadn't told him because she didn't feel she could.

His stomach lurched as another thought came to him. What if she hadn't told him because she wasn't planning on going through with it? What if she and Ethan had gone to the hospital to ask about a termination? What if they were there for the procedure?

He looked at his watch. Almost half an hour had passed. Would he be too late? Should he call her, tell her he knew, ask her not to go through with it? Was that what he wanted? More importantly, was it what she wanted? Would she even be able to do that without parental consent? He wasn't sure how it worked. He had a horrifying thought that Emily had told the hospital her parents were dead or estranged. But wouldn't they then need to speak to whoever her legal guardian was? Another terrible thought hit him. What if she hadn't gone to Jack because, instead, she'd gone to Helen? Was his ex-wife inside the hospital with Emily now? The ex-wife who abandoned them both, dumped Emily with her grandparents and went off to drink the world dry?

He needed to clear his head. He couldn't work like this. Didn't want to, in any case. All he wanted was to be there to comfort Emily.

Above all, he felt guilty. Guilty that he couldn't be there for her. Guilty that she hadn't come to him. Guilty that Ethan Turner, the lowest scrote of them all, had bothered to turn up at the hospital first thing in the morning to embrace Emily and take her hand, accompanying her into the maternity wing. He hadn't even done that himself when Helen had fallen pregnant with Emily. He didn't make it to a single antenatal class. Not one midwife's appointment. Work had always got in the way.

If he was honest with himself, that was at the root of everything. That cold, lifeless grey building in front of him. That lump of concrete with rising damp. He'd spent his life trying to put criminals behind bars, and as a result he'd found himself second-best to one of them, a petty thief proving to be a better father than he'd ever been.

In any case, years of neglect couldn't be undone in a single morning. There was very little that could be done about his personal life right now, but his career was, he hoped, still salvageable. Jack got out of his car and walked into the station, making his way through the maze of corridors and up into his office.

Before his backside had hit the chair, his phone rang. It was Charles Hawes.

'Jack, can you pop up to my office please?' the Chief Constable said. 'And bring Detective Sergeant Knight with you.'

Jack and Wendy both knew instinctively what it would be about. They were being pulled in to get roasted over the visit they'd paid to Theo, without informing or getting authorisation from Professional Standards.

'I'm not going to beat around the bush,' Hawes said once the pair had entered his office and sat down. 'The death of PC Curwood is going to cause us a lot of problems, from a lot of angles. Now, I know it can't have been easy finding him like that...'

'I've seen plenty of stiffs in my time, sir,' Jack said.

'I understand that. But my primary concern right now is for my officers. There was no way in hell you should have even been there. Professional Standards have full responsibility for the investigation into PC Curwood. You know that. This really does not look good, Jack. You're going to have a lot of questions to answer.'

'With respect, sir, we needed to speak to him. He was the missing link between the robberies and the people responsible. Between you and me, I don't think PC Curwood was a bad egg. I think his head was turned by money. And I think I know who turned it.'

'Again, that's PS's job. They've got the ability to do far more than we can, and that enables them to uncover the whole tangled web. We can't just go thundering in like a bull in a china shop. Now the whole lot of them will have been spooked, and there's fuck all we can do. They'll have gone to ground. Burned their bridges.'

Jack wondered how many idioms and clichés the Chief could fit into a single speech.

'Sir, I've got to say, it was done with the best of intentions,' Wendy said, trying to defend Jack.

'It doesn't bloody matter what your intentions were, Detective Sergeant Knight. Professional Standards will be all over this, and they're going to think you were involved. They'll think you were trying to cover something up. There are corrupt officers in the force, one is identified and then two others rock up at his place and find him hanging from the ceiling. Do you have any idea how that's going to look?'

'With respect, sir, he'd been dead for hours when we found him.'

'I know that, and you know that. But that's not how it'll be dressed up. You're a pair of fucking idiots, the both of you.'

'Sorry, sir,' Jack said. 'But that's wrong. DS Knight had no part to play in this. She tried convincing me not to get involved. She warned me it'd mean picking a fight with Professional Standards. The worst she did was reluctantly agree to allow me to make a phone call to Theo, and she didn't even want me to do that. She's not to blame. I am.'

Hawes sat back in his chair and folded his arms across his chest, seemingly happy enough with Jack's comments.

'You know Penny Andrews is going to be all over this, don't you Jack?'

'Yeah. Well you can give her a message from me.'

'What's that?' the Chief Constable asked.

'Tell her to go fuck herself.'

37

Jack and Wendy walked silently back to the incident room, with the only spoken words being Wendy's thanks to Jack for defending her. He nodded his acceptance, then went into his office and shut the door behind him.

He didn't know which way to turn. He had plenty of people to make up to, and a number of decisions to be made. One of them was simple enough, though.

He took his phone out of his pocket and called Chrissie. He glanced at his watch, noting that she'd be at work, but hoping she might be on her own in the office and able to take his call. After thirty seconds or so, his call went through to voicemail.

'Hi Chrissie. It's me,' he said. 'Look, I just wanted to ring you to apologise for not getting back to you the other day. Some stuff's kicked off at work and at... Well, at work. And I just wanted to say sorry I hadn't been in touch and didn't answer you. That's about it really. Sorry. Call me when you get this, please.'

He put his phone down on the desk and leaned back in his chair, resting his head against the leather. He could easily sleep now. Push everything out of his mind and get an hour's peace. But he knew there was no way that was going to happen.

As if reading his mind, there was a knock at the door and Wendy entered. She didn't say anything at first, but came and sat on the corner of his desk.

'Seriously,' she said. 'Thanks. You didn't need to do that.'

'Yeah I know. I did it because I'm the best boss you're ever going to have, or anybody could ever wish to have.'

'Something like that. But I don't want you to be my boss at the moment. I want you to be my colleague. My... acquaintance. What's wrong? You've been distant the last couple of days, and on a completely different planet this morning.'

Jack exhaled heavily. 'Fuck, where do I start?'

'Give me the headlines.'

He thought for a moment, wondering whether to skirt around the issue or dive straight in.

'It's Emily. I think she might be pregnant.'

Wendy struggled to hide her surprise. 'Wow. Okay.'

'Yeah. And I'm pretty sure the father is known to us.'

'Blimey. Yeah, I can see why that might play on your mind a bit. Have you spoken to her about it?'

Jack shook his head. 'She doesn't know I know. I only really found out this morning. I mean, I think I've probably known for a couple of days, deep down. The other morning when I went in the bathroom I could tell she'd been sick in there. Sounds stupid to say it, but I just hoped it was underage drinking or drugs or something.'

'Is there anything I can do to help?' Wendy asked.

'I doubt it, to be honest. I don't even know what I can do.'

'Maybe you should sit down and have a chat with her. Calmly, I mean. In a supportive way. Or I could do it, if you like? Might be easier with a woman.'

'She barely knows you.'

'I know. That might be an advantage. Although, if you want me to change the subject entirely, I've got something that might cheer you up. That private security firm Ian Gumbert hired after the robberies? The one that Theo Curwood recommended to him? One of the shareholders is Gary McCann.'

'Yeah, I already guessed that one. I appreciate the senti-ment, though.'

'Alright. In that case, what if I told you we'd done a bit of digging into their employees and discovered that there's a disproportionately high number of ex-cons working for them. Three of them were in the same prison as Damian King. At the same time. One of them was a cellmate of his.'

Jack looked up at Wendy. 'Are you serious?'

'Oh yes,' she said. 'Deadly serious.'

38

The new breakthrough had given them more than enough to re-arrest Damian King. There was now something else linking him to the robberies — the fact that he'd shared a cell with one of the employees of the security company who'd weaselled their way into looking after Ian Gumbert's petrol stations, and that two further employees had been in the same prison at the same time.

It was starting to come together, and on the face of it everything looked very simple. There was something nagging at Jack, though. McCann was a clever bugger, and it had seemed a little easy and convenient that he was listed as a director or shareholder at the security firm and the locks and glazing company that fitted Elsie Fogg's new back door. That was a clear paper trail, of sorts. Of course, a decent solicitor would argue — probably successfully — that this was purely a coincidence. Gary McCann had fingers in a huge number of pies, and had directorships at a large percentage of local businesses. That was what he did.

If that was the case, it infuriated Jack. It was almost as if McCann was dangling this right under his nose, knowing Jack would see the truth but be unable to do anything about it. That was always the case with McCann — he almost went out of his way to make sure Jack knew he was involved, but was wise enough to ensure the evidence was only ever circumstantial at best. Just a little hint here and there, but never anything they could come anywhere near being able to do anything about. One day, Jack knew McCann would drop the ball. And he'd be there, ready and waiting to volley the fucker into next week.

Jack and Wendy were back in his office, preparing their approach for Damian King's interview. He'd been arrested at his home and brought in, and was currently being booked into the custody suite. They'd had to apply for an extension to detain him, as there were only a few minutes left on his custody clock from his previous arrest. They'd got an extension to thirty-six hours, giving them just over twelve to either charge or release him.

'Listen, before we get stuck in I just wanted to say thanks for earlier,' Jack said.

'How do you mean?'

'For listening. Checking on me. Whatever. Just wanted to say thanks.'

'It's fine. My pleasure.'

'And how are you?' he asked.

Wendy was a little taken aback. She was pretty sure this was the first time he'd ever asked after anyone else's welfare, especially hers. 'Yeah, fine thanks.'

'And things with Xav? They good?'

'Yeah, they are,' she said, smiling. 'Apart from him bugging me to take the inspector's exam again.'

'He's got a point. You'd absolutely smash it, if you ask me. You're good. But don't let that get to your head, alright?'

Wendy smiled again. 'I'll try. I dunno, though. I still haven't decided.'

'What's holding you back?'

'Honestly? My dad.'

'Your dad's dead.'

'Exactly. He never got to achieve what he wanted to achieve. His career was cut short at Inspector level. I dunno. I kind of feel as if I'd be doing him a disservice if I reach what he reached, or even go beyond that. He had no choice. It was taken away from him. It feels wrong somehow.'

Jack swallowed. 'Every parent wants their kids to do better than they did. To have more opportunities than they did. And I know damn well your dad was no different. He'd have wanted you to reach for the stars.'

Wendy tried to hold back the tears. 'I know he would.'

'Right. That's sorted then. Now, onto nailing this King fucker.'

. . .

The interview started much as they'd suspected, although this time Damian had opted to have a solicitor present. He was clearly smart enough to know that if they'd re-arrested him and got authority to add more time to his custody clock, they must have something on him. Jack and Wendy were thankful for the solicitor's presence, as it seemed to at least mute Damian's arrogance somewhat.

'Damian, do you mind if we ask you again where you were on these dates?' Wendy asked, referring to the nights of the robberies.

'I believe my client has already answered that question in a previous interview,' the solicitor said, speaking for Damian.

'That's correct, but we're asking him again.'

'You can ask all you like, but he has no obligation to answer. He's provided you with full alibis, I understand.'

Wendy looked at King. 'Damian?'

'No comment,' he said, with a small sneer.

'Listen, Damian,' Jack said, leaning forward. 'We're not interested in your silly little games, not that it matters anymore anyway. We know you used to work at Ian Gumbert's petrol station. We know you hated Gumbert. We know you stole from him. We know you've got form for violent assault. We know you visited Fogg's Jewellers and you even provided us with a nice alibi from a prostitute to corroborate that fact. And that's not all. Detective Sergeant Knight?'

'Tell us about your time at HMP Bathurst, Damian.'

'What about it?'

'Any particular friends you made? Cellmates, perhaps?'

'A few. Can't avoid that in prison, though, can you? Not many other places to go. It's sort of the point.'

'Do you recognise any of these gentlemen from your time at Her Majesty's pleasure?' Wendy asked, opening a folder and passing three photos across the desk to Damian.

'You don't have to answer,' the solicitor said.

Damian looked up at them. 'I don't have to answer.'

'That's fine,' Wendy said. 'I can answer the question for you. This one here is Ezekiel Copeland, who was serving time for extortion on the same wing as you. The chap next to him is Tyler O'Dowd. He was in for stealing his own nan's life savings, believe it or not. She'd had enough of his antics and reported him to the police. Unfortunately for him it was fourth time unlucky, and he spent a short period of time inside HMP Bathurst, on... Oh yes. The same wing as you. And the handsome gentleman next to him is Angelo Soanes. Do you know him a bit better, perhaps?'

'No comment.'

'That's rather odd, because we have it on good authority he was your cellmate.'

'Don't have a very good memory for faces, do you?' Jack asked.

'You don't need to respond,' the solicitor told Damian.

'These three gentlemen now all work for the same security company in Mildenheath. That company came to Ian Gumbert following the robberies he was a victim of, offering to keep his premises secure. That's the Ian Gumbert you used to work for, in the petrol station that was robbed, who you hated and stole money from.'

'Maybe we should take a break there so my client and I can liaise in private,' the solicitor said, going to stand up.

'No,' King said. 'No, let's do this. Let's roll. Come on. Give it to me.'

'Alright,' Wendy said. 'Maybe you could tell us a little more about how all these little pieces fall into place.'

'No comment,' Damian said, smirking.

'From where I'm sitting, Damian,' Jack said, 'it looks as if you're the mastermind behind this operation. Of course, we both know that isn't true because you're thick as pig shit, but that doesn't really matter. As things stand, you're the only one we have something on so you're the one who's going to take the rap unless you man up and tell us what's been going on, who's involved and who's behind this operation.'

The solicitor leaned forward. 'Detective Chief Inspector, I really feel we must—'

'Shut up,' Damian said. 'Just shut up, alright?'

'You're the boss,' the solicitor murmured, leaning back in his chair and folding his arms across his chest.

'Look, all I know is some people were approached to do some jobs for someone and they asked me to join them. I said no.'

'Why's that?' Jack asked.

'Cos I'm sick of working for tossers.'

'I had no idea you and I were so similar, Damian. We've bonded at last.'

'Look, I didn't want to go back inside, alright? You know what it's like in there. People give it all that, but it's fucking shit. There's no-one who actually likes it, no matter what they say. No easy cash is getting me back in there.'

'Who approached you, Damian?'

'A mate.'

'What's his name?'

'I'm not telling you. He's not connected to all this.'

'Is he one of the three men we showed you earlier?'

'I just said I'm not telling you, alright?' Damian's voice was growing in volume.

'How does it feel to be a grass, Damian?' Jack asked, spotting the chink in the man's armour.

King looked visibly angry. 'Fuck off. Get out of my fucking face.'

The solicitor leaned forward again. 'Detectives, I really think perhaps we should take a short interlude to—'

'Absolutely correct,' Culverhouse said, cutting him off. 'Interview terminated.'

Jack and Wendy stepped outside the interview room, leaving Damian King and his brief to their own devices.

'Speak to the custody sergeant and get him bailed,' Jack said.

'Seriously?'

'Seriously. We've got fuck all else right now. We need to get the custody clock stopped before we waste any more time. You and I both know what happens next. We let him go, he goes back home and panics. He calls whoever the mate was who tried to get him involved. He'll make contact. He has to. Get his calls and texts tracked. I'll arrange covert surveillance of his home.'

'How? You'll never get authorisation for that.'

'I don't need authorisation to stick a couple of fat fucks in a Vauxhall Vectra for the night. If they happen to spend it looking at Damian King's front door, there's nothing illegal about that either.'

Wendy chuckled inwardly. She knew exactly who Jack was talking about based on his description of them, and she hoped Steve and Frank didn't have any plans for the evening.

39

That evening, Jack sat on his sofa, staring at the television. It was showing some sort of documentary about the history of TV game shows, but he wasn't really watching. His mind was elsewhere.

He'd managed to talk Steve and Frank into staking out Damian's place tonight. It was the sort of operation which would usually require special authority, but Jack wasn't one to worry about due procedure. In any case, it didn't have to be official. What was wrong with two blokes sitting in a car all night if they wanted to? The only worry would be that any evidence obtained might not be admissible in court, but they could worry about that later. There were ways and means.

In any case, that wasn't the main thing on his mind right now. Emily was upstairs in her room. He imagined she'd be doing what she usually did — either watching TV or listening to music with her headphones on while she texted friends or played games on her phone.

He knew he needed to bring up the subject of the hospital visit — of her pregnancy — but he didn't know how. His natural instinct, as always, was to be direct. The standard Jack Culverhouse response would be to barge in, get straight to the point and tell her how it was. But even he knew that approach didn't always work — and certainly not with Emily.

Being subtle was difficult for Jack, though. He wasn't the most subtle person in any conceivable way. And anyway, how on earth could he be subtle while bringing up a subject like this? It wasn't possible. Not for him.

His third option, as he saw it, was to give her the space and opportunity to come to him. His biggest worry was that she hadn't felt able to confide in him already. That was hardly surprising, seeing as she'd spent the vast majority of her life away from him and had only come back into his life relatively recently. But it still hurt.

He wondered if perhaps he could drop a few hints somehow. Maybe touch on the fact he was proud of her growing up into a young woman, and that she'd almost certainly meet challenges and life changes along the way, but that he'd always be there for her. To him, though, that sounded too much like heavy hinting. And, in any case, it definitely didn't sound like him.

While he was mulling this over, Emily came downstairs

and into the living room. Jack noticed she was carrying a rucksack.

'Alright?' he said, more due to a lack of other conversational ideas than anything else.

'Yeah, fine. I was thinking of going to stay at a friend's place tonight, if that's alright.'

Jack looked at the rucksack, knowing she'd done more than just think about it. She was ready to go. 'Oh right. Which friend?'

'Oh, you don't know her. She's having boyfriend trouble.'

Jack nodded. 'Well, she's more than welcome to come over here if she likes. Change of scenery might help. I can put the camp bed up in here.'

'I think she just wants to be at home, really.'

'Right. Okay. Look, I wondered if we could have a chat, actually. There's something I need to speak to you about. Is there any chance you might be able to stay in, and I can drop you over to hers in the morning instead?'

'I dunno,' Emily said. 'She really needs me. She's got a bit of a history of harming herself and stuff, so I think it's for the best that I go. She seemed to really want me to. Practically begged me, in fact.'

Jack thought about this for a moment, and nodded slowly. 'Alright. Well, how about I drop you over there? It'll save you walking and it means we can at least have a chat in the car. I mean, it's not ideal, but it's better than nothing I suppose.'

Emily contorted her face and shook her head. 'Nah, I could do with the fresh air. Anyway, it's not far. Just round the corner, really. In fact, I should probably get going.'

Emily reached for the door handle, and Jack's heart lurched.

'I know you're going to see Ethan, Emily.'

There were seconds of silence, during which Jack realised he'd been holding his breath. He desperately tried to gauge Emily's reaction from the back of her head, and wondered for a moment if he'd managed to throw it all away.

'How?' came the eventual whispered reply.

'I just do. It's my job to know when people are hiding things, no matter how well they think they're hiding it.'

'What, and you think I'm the same as one of the criminals you deal with at work? You think I'm trying to hide something from you? Go on, then. What is it? What am I trying to hide?'

'Emily, this isn't the time or the place.'

'Yes it is. You were the one who wanted me to stay in and have a chat thirty seconds ago. So come on. What did you want to talk about? Was it this? Was it Ethan?'

'In a manner of speaking.'

Emily held eye contact with Jack. She could clearly see something in his eyes, and Jack could see in hers that she'd noticed. They were straying too close to the truth for her to go any further, and Jack knew he had to be the one to take control of this situation.

'Look, Em, I know you think parents are daft old duffers who don't know anything about life, but I've been there. Trust me, it only feels like yesterday I was your age. I remember everything. I know how it feels. I know the things that go on. I didn't live in Victorian times, you know.'

Emily's voice was almost a whisper. 'I don't know what you're talking about.'

'Em, listen. I know. The mood changes. Being ill. Forgetting things. And... And you were seen going into the hospital yesterday morning. With Ethan.'

Emily's face flushed white as he spoke. 'Who?'

'What?'

'Who saw me?'

'That doesn't matter.'

'Yes it does. No-one you know even knows what I look like, other than Chrissie and she was at school. It was you, wasn't it?'

'Wendy Knight knows what you look like too.'

'Was it her?'

Jack swallowed. 'No.'

He could see the tears welling in Emily's eyes as she nodded her acceptance, knowing implicitly what had gone on.

'You had no right to do that,' she said, her voice breaking as the tears began to cascade down her cheeks. 'This is my life, Dad.'

'I know that. Trust me, I do. And I'm a part of it. I'm your Dad. You should be able to tell me these things.'

Emily snorted. 'Are you serious? You follow me around town and spy on me, then reckon I should use you as some sort of shoulder to cry on? You're fucking crazy.'

'Em, I didn't spy on you.'

'Sounds like it to me.'

Jack stood up and walked towards her, trying to embrace her.

'Get away from me!' Emily stepped back, closer to the door, and Jack did as he was told. He had no desire to push her away any further.

'Em, come on. Let's talk. I'm not angry, I promise.'

'Well I fucking am! Do you want to know something? Do you want to know someone who doesn't treat me like this? Ethan. He's been solid. He's looked after me every step of the way. So don't you *dare* talk to me about being there for me.'

As Jack's heart sunk in his chest, he watched as Emily closed the door behind her and strode purposefully down the driveway towards the road.

40

Damian had spotted the two coppers straight away. The fat bastards didn't exactly blend into their surroundings, no matter how much they thought they did.

He'd thought about waving to them as he walked past, but decided against it. That'd only spook them into disappearing and trying something else. It'd be much funnier to let them sit out there in the freezing cold all night, thinking they were James Bond and Jason Bourne.

He peered out of his bedroom window and down onto the street below, and could see two fat bellies through the windscreen of their car. He wanted to laugh, but was keen not to create too much movement. He didn't want them to know he'd seen them.

He was standing a few feet back from the window, with the lights off, so he was fairly sure they hadn't spotted him. It was just over three hours ago that he got home, so they'd been sitting there at least that long — probably longer. He kind of felt sorry for them, in a way. He decided he was going to have a bit of fun.

He went downstairs, put on his shoes and opened the front door. Having closed it behind him, he walked down the short path, opened the gate and headed off down the road. When he got to the car with the police officers in it, he stopped and knocked on the side window. After a second or two, the window was wound down.

'Evening, officers. Bit cold out tonight, so I just wondered if you'd like a cup of tea or a choccy biscuit?'

The fat fucks looked stunned. They didn't know what to say. Damian decided to come to their rescue.

'Actually, don't worry about it. You don't have to. Just thought I would ask 'cos I'm off to bed now. It's that one up there, by the way. The one with the flag in the window. Pop a note through the door if you want Weetabix for the morning, yeah?'

Damian smacked his hand playfully on the roof of the car a couple of times, beaming from ear to ear as he walked back to his house. That should shit them up. Stupid twats, thinking they know it all.

He let himself back in, sat down on a kitchen chair and took off his ankle tag. He didn't see the point in the things, personally. They were a piece of piss to get round. It wasn't even a game any more; it was almost boring.

He put on a jacket, opened the back door and let himself out into the garden. At the end of the garden he unlatched the gate and stepped out onto the public foot-path. Of course, they had no-one watching the back of the house. That'd be too easy for them. They liked to make life difficult for themselves. Twats.

Even though they'd done a shit job of it, Damian was still pissed off that they'd even tried. They were hell bent on trying to fit him up for it. It didn't matter how many alibis he gave them, nor how good his brief was. He didn't know what they hoped to get out of it. Did they think he was going to slip up or decide he'd had enough and admit to everything? They were idiots if they did.

He was protected. He was untouchable. If only those clowns knew what was going on, they'd know there was no way in hell they were able to pin anything on anyone. And even if they did, they'd be taking themselves down with it. It'd be like a three-way fire fight, with everyone pointing their gun at the bloke on their left. There were only two ways it could end: everyone quietly walked away, or everyone went down with the ship. And they had far more to lose than he did.

Even so, it frustrated the fuck out of him. There was no way he was going to sleep with those fat bastards sitting outside. If only he could drop the big one, there was no way they'd keep pestering him. They'd have no choice but to leave him alone. But he couldn't. Not yet. That frustrated him.

He vaulted the wall onto Windermere Street and looked both ways down the road. He walked a little further down, then crossed and headed up a side alley, before knocking on the door of 23a.

The door opened a few seconds later, and he stepped inside. The ambience was just as he knew it, and he could already feel the stirrings inside him.

'Good evening, Damian,' the man said.

'Alright. Is she in?'

'She's not, actually. But I was hoping you might pop in. We've got a new girl for you. Very high class. Someone I think you're going to like.'

Damian wasn't sure. He'd always had the same woman, had grown attached to her. He hadn't planned on proposing to her for nothing. 'I dunno. Might just be easier if I come back another time. When's she in?'

The man shrugged. 'I don't know. But I promise you, this new girl is super special. Trust me. First time's on the house. Just so you can see exactly what you're missing out on.'

Damian smiled. 'On the house?'

'Absolutely. And if you don't come out of there an hour later with an even bigger smile on your face, you can have her for nothing any time you like.'

Damian couldn't help but grin. Things were starting to look up.

41

Jack's eyes were once again transfixed on the television, but taking in none of it. He'd been desperate to go after Emily, but knew it would only make things worse. In any case, he knew where she was. She'd be at Ethan's house. He could almost guarantee it.

He stood up from his chair, walked into the kitchen and took a bottle of white wine out of the fridge, pouring himself a glass large enough to keep him happy but small enough to ensure he could still drive if he needed to.

When he got back in the living room, he noticed his mobile phone vibrating on the arm of the sofa. It was Frank Vine.

'Yes, Frank,' he said, answering.

'Bit of a problem, guv,' Frank said. 'We've been spotted.'

'What do you mean you've been spotted?'

'I mean he walked straight out of his house, bold as brass and came over to the car. He called us out.'

'Fuck's sake. Where's he gone now?'

'To bed.'

'To bed?'

'So he says, yeah.'

'Jesus Christ, Frank. How the hell did you two manage to fuck that up? All you had to do was sit in a car and look inconspicuous.'

'Yeah, well it's not easy to do round here. It's more difficult than it sounds.'

Jack let out a sigh. 'I'm pretty sure you two would say the same about breathing. Right, well you might as well knock off. No point you sticking around. He's hardly likely to give us anything now he knows you're sitting outside, is he?'

Jack hung up the phone and sat down on the sofa, taking a large mouthful of wine. No sooner had he done so, his phone rang again. He half expected it was Frank ringing back and was about to answer the phone with a string of expletives before realising it was Chrissie.

'I got your voicemail,' she said.

It took him a few seconds to realise what she was talking about. He couldn't recall a voicemail. But then he remembered having called her to apologise for not getting back to her the other night.

'Don't worry about it,' he said. 'It's fine.'

'Good. That's pretty much what I was ringing you to say, too.'

'Then everything's fine.'

'Yep.'

'Good.'

'Good,' Chrissie said.

Jack took a deep breath. 'Listen, today's been shit. Do you fancy heading over here to keep me company? Nothing saucy. I just fancy having someone else around.'

'Haven't you got Emily?'

'No. Long story, that one.'

'Oh right. Well, I can't really. Sorry.' Chrissie's voice sounded different, as if she was thinking about something entirely different.

'What have I done?' he asked.

'You? Nothing.'

'So why are you being weird?'

'I'm not,' she said.

'Chrissie, come on. I've had enough of people being off with me today. I don't know if there's something in the water, or what. Just tell me what's up.'

Chrissie stayed silent for a few seconds before speaking. 'I can't come over, Jack. Something happened.'

The way in which she said it made Jack's heart lurch.

'Like what?' he asked.

'I'm in hospital,' she said. 'I was attacked.'

42

Jack drove to the hospital as quickly as he legally could. She'd asked him not to, but there was no way he was going to listen to that.

She hadn't given him many details — just that she was walking back to her car in the school car park after work and had been set upon by two men. She said she was fine — just a bit bruised — but had accidentally let slip that they'd also managed to break her leg.

Uniformed officers had already attended and taken a statement, but Jack wasn't visiting on official police business — not that he told the ward sister that.

He showed her his police identification and asked which bed Chrissie was in, before following the instructions to take the second room on the left, where he'd find her in bed six. Visiting hours were long over, and this was the only way he'd be able to get to see her before tomorrow.

Bed six did at least have a window view, not that it mattered much as it was now dark and, in any case, the view was of Mildenheath.

Chrissie was asleep, so Jack nudged her gently awake.

'Jack? What are you doing here?'

'I've come to see you, you daft cow. You dropped off to sleep pretty quick, didn't you? I was only on the phone to you ten minutes ago.'

'It's these painkillers,' she said, wincing as she tried to make herself more comfortable.

'Are they good?'

'Define "good". They don't do anything for the pain, but they definitely stop me giving a shit.'

'I reckon I could do with a few of those myself. How are you feeling?'

'Like I've been decked by two blokes in a car park.'

Jack let out a deep sigh. 'Yeah. I can imagine. Did you manage to get a look at them?'

Chrissie shook her head. 'A colleague of yours already took a statement. Uniform. Rashid, I think his name was.'

'Think I know the one,' Jack said, the name ringing a vague bell at the back of his mind from a previous case. 'What are we looking at? Black clothing and balaclavas, I suppose?'

'I honestly don't know. I didn't see them. By the time I knew what was happening, I was face-down on the ground and they were running away.'

'Anything nicked?'

'No. That's the weirdest thing about it. They left my handbag and my car keys, which I had in my hand. They didn't take a thing.'

Jack knew this wasn't a coincidence. They were sending him a message. 'Probably just drunken yobs,' he said.

'Look, I'm sorry about the Emily thing. I know we both said it was fine, but I should have mentioned something sooner.'

'No,' Jack replied, shaking his head. 'You did the right thing not to get involved. I shouldn't have reacted the way I did. It's... There's probably a few things me and Emily need to talk about. And we'll probably need to loop you in on that, too.'

'As her headteacher or as... Well, as whatever else you'd call me.'

'Hop-along?' he said, gesturing towards her leg.

Chrissie laughed, then winced again at the pain of doing so. 'I was thinking more "significant other", but I'll take what I can get.'

Jack's face turned serious again. 'You know what? You have a right to know. Whether it's as her headteacher or as my... hop-along. There's a reason she's been late to school and why she's been distant. She's pregnant.'

'Oh wow. Okay. It might be these drugs, but I'm going to have to make you repeat that.'

'Yeah. I had much the same response, except for the

drugs bit. Wouldn't have minded being smacked off my tits when that bombshell dropped, I tell you.'

'How did it go down? Did she just come out and tell you?'

Jack shuffled awkwardly. 'Not exactly.'

'You spied on her, didn't you.'

'I found out of my own accord, if that's what you mean.'

Chrissie, in her own inimitable way, continued without judgement. 'How did she react?'

'How do you think?'

'Loudly.'

'That's pretty much it, yeah. She made me out to be the villain for wanting to support her. I just don't know what to do, Chrissie. It's all fucking up around me.'

'Well, first of all you can stop moping. At least you can walk. And see out of both eyes. This is your chance to be a good dad to her. She won't see it at the moment because it's all fresh and dramatic, and she's hormonal. But give her a bit of space and let her know you're there for her. She needs a support network right now. It's a huge moment for her.'

'It's huge for me too.'

'My sister had a baby when she was young,' Chrissie said, staring off into the middle distance. 'Sixteen, she was. It totally changed her life and her relationship with our mum and dad. She was sort of elevated to being their equal, in a way. It was like she had to step forward and move into that next stage of life. This could be Emily's chance to get some sort of grounding in life.'

'I know. I get that.'

'You've got to keep your arms open to her, Jack.'

'I'm trying. But whatever I do, I seem to just keep pushing people away. I don't even do it on purpose. I just... I dunno. Maybe that's why I never get close to people. Look what happens when I do. You got too close and you've ended up in here. I'm bad news, Chrissie. Where I go, stuff falls apart. Trust me, I'll totally understand if you want to get away from me. I wouldn't blame you one bit. It'd probably be the best thing for you.'

'Jack, listen to me,' Chrissie said, her face stern. 'I'm going nowhere, alright? I'm a big girl now. I can stand up for myself. On two legs, eventually. You need to stop worrying, stop looking backwards and do just one thing.'

Jack looked up at her, holding back his tears. 'What's that?' he asked.

Chrissie pointed to her leg. 'You go out there and catch the bastards who did this.'

43

Damian King was having the time of his life. The guy out front had been spot on — this girl was the bomb!

The basement room was usually reserved for high-paying clients or multi-person events. Damian had never been down there before, but he could see why people paid good money for it.

There was all sorts of bizarre apparatus hanging from the walls and ceilings. Damian wasn't interested in using it — it wasn't really his scene — but the girl, who'd introduced herself as Sylvia, was keen to experiment with him.

'I hear you've been a naughty little boy,' Sylvia said, whispering softly into his ear as she played with his manhood.

'Oh yeah,' Damian replied between groans of pleasure. 'Very naughty.'

'In that case, I think I need to tie you to my special board.'

'I'm... Mmm, I'm not usually a fan of being tied up,' Damian said, struggling to get the words out as he glanced down at what she was doing.

'Oh I think you're going to like this,' she said. 'Besides which, it's what you deserve for being a naughty little boy.'

She tightened her grip slightly, making Damian moan in ecstasy. 'Yes, miss. Whatever you say, miss.'

'Good boy,' she whispered, her breath hot on his neck, sending shivers down his spine.

She led him over to the far wall and stood him on a small platform, before tying his arms up above his head and binding his ankles beneath him.

A million and one thoughts went through Damian's mind. He couldn't help but admit he was getting even more turned on by being tied up here, stark naked, completely at the whim of whatever Sylvia wanted to do to him. And he wanted her to do a *lot* to him.

'Oh god,' he said. 'You're definitely my new favourite. I need to see you more. All the time. God. Fuck.'

He felt a bit bad about letting down the woman he wanted to marry, but women were ten a penny. If this one liked him as much as he liked her, she was a keeper. He could do this a thousand times over. A million. The money didn't matter.

'Now you know what naughty little boys get, don't

you?' Sylvia said, bending down beside the apparatus and reaching into a bag.

'N... No miss.'

'They get punished.'

'Y... Yes miss.'

Before Damian could realise what was happening, Sylvia raised the gun and dispatched two bullets between his eyes.

44

Jack Culverhouse wasn't in the business of letting people down, and that sense of responsibility was never greater than with those close to him. Few people had got truly close to him over the years, but that didn't mean he didn't care for them. And when it came to Emily and Chrissie, he felt ultra-protective.

Chrissie was safe for now. That could be dealt with in the fresh light of day tomorrow. For now, he had other, more pressing business to take care of.

Jack had committed Ethan Turner's address to memory after looking him up again on the Police National Computer earlier that day. He'd moved since Jack had last searched for his address, to a flat on a grotty estate Jack'd had the misfortune of visiting a number of times throughout his career.

He drove over there straight from the hospital, parking

his car on the edge of the estate in an area he reasoned might at least be verging on safe, and walked the rest of the way.

When he found the right building, he opened the front door and made his way up to the third floor, where flat nine was situated. A flat on the ground floor was either having a party or doing a good job of pissing off the neighbours, the heavy bassline of the music pounding through the building. A couple on the first floor were having a blazing row in an Eastern European language. The third floor seemed relatively calm in comparison, but it was fair to say it was a shithole.

Jack didn't know who had responsibility in cleaning the building, but it was pretty clear no-one was stepping up to the mark. It looked as if the floor hadn't been mopped in months, and the rising damp on the walls showed a distinct lack of care and maintenance. There was no way a baby could be brought up in these conditions. But, at the same time, there seemed to be no way Emily would return to him without something drastic happening.

He knocked gingerly on the door, determined to see his daughter and clear the air, but also nervous as to what he might find — and how he might react.

A few seconds later, the door opened, and Ethan Turner was in front of him, recognising Jack immediately and clearly a little surprised, even though he tried not to show it.

'What do you want?' Turner said, turning on the big boy act.

'I want to speak to Emily,' Jack replied, keeping as calm as he could.

'She don't want to speak to you. How'd you find this place?'

Jack rolled his eyes. 'I'm a police officer, Ethan. It's my job to find things.'

Ethan's body language stiffened, almost as if he didn't know that crucial piece of information about him.

Jack tried to calm the atmosphere. 'Listen, I'm not here on police business. None of that bothers me right now. I'm not interested in anything else except Emily.'

'What, you trying to say I'm doing illegal stuff and you're just gonna ignore it? What proof you got?' Ethan said, taking a step forward, hoping to rile Jack into attacking.

'I'm not saying anything of the sort. I'm saying I'm here to speak to Emily, as her father. I don't have any beef with you, and I'm not here to pick a fight. I want to clear the air with her.'

At that moment, he saw Emily step into the corridor behind Ethan. She'd been crying, but didn't say a word.

'She don't want to talk to you, bruv,' Ethan said.

Jack looked over his shoulder to his daughter. 'Em?'

'Mate, don't ignore me,' Ethan said, taking another step forward until he was nose to nose with Jack. 'This is my fucking flat, yeah? You talk to me, yeah?'

'Ethan, leave it,' Emily said, taking his hand and tugging him gently backwards. 'Please. Let me just talk to him for a couple of minutes, then he'll be gone.'

Ethan didn't break eye contact with Jack, but slowly nodded. 'Alright. But the cunt ain't coming in here. He stays out there on the landing with the other rats.'

Ethan turned and walked back down the corridor and off into a side room, slamming the door behind him. Jack was now face to face with his daughter.

'Em, I'm sorry. I could come up with a million excuses or try to justify it, but that won't change anything. All that matters is that I'm sorry. Trust me, I just want to help.'

'By spying on me?'

'I said sorry. Look, I just want us to be a family. You have no idea how much it meant to me when you came back into my life. I had every emotion under the sun, but all that mattered were the good ones. It felt like I'd been given a second chance. You have no idea how much I've spent every single day regretting the way things were before you and your mum left. I have to throw myself into my work, because otherwise I spend every second wondering how I could have done things differently. It's eating away at me. But when you came back, I had another shot at things. And trust me, I've done everything to make sure I don't fuck it up again. I couldn't handle it if that happened. I know I fucked up massively as a dad, but I am *not* going to fuck up as a grandad as well. I know I reacted badly, but believe me, I just wanted to help.

You're fifteen. I was just being protective. It's kind of my job.'

'Not by following me. Or smothering me.'

'Em, it's going to take me a bit of time to get the balance right. Don't forget I spent years doing nothing for you. Not even knowing you. Maybe I'm overcompensating now. I apologise for that. But I really am doing my best. I need you to tell me when I go too far, so we can make this work for both of us.'

Jack watched as a tear rolled down Emily's face. As he was about to step forward into the doorway to hug her, he heard the sound of a door opening and Ethan marched back out into the corridor.

'Right, that's your two minutes,' he said. 'Get out of here.'

'Please Em,' Jack said, ignoring Ethan. 'I mean it all.'

'She'll think about it,' Ethan said, putting his hand high on the doorframe and leaning against it, blocking Jack's line of sight to Emily.

Jack fought back the overwhelming urge to sink his fist into the skinny fucker's face and break every bone in his skull. But he knew he had to swallow his pride. If he overreacted now, he'd just prove Emily's point and send her running back to Ethan. If he left with his pride on the floor, there was still a chance she might come back to him. He had to let her trust him.

Jack looked at the floor, took a deep breath then headed back down the stairs towards the street.

45

Cyril Copeland drew in deep lungfuls of the crisp morning air as he marched across Mildenheath Common after Bongo.

The dog was having a whale of time, as well he might after five days without a walk. Cyril was starting to feel a slight twinge in his ankle occasionally, but it was pretty well strapped up and the doctor had told him he could go back to walking Bongo from this morning onwards.

His ankle wasn't the only thing that seemed to be improving. The gurgling in his intestines told him the most awkward effect of the painkillers he'd been given was starting to wear off. Fortunately, he'd only been on them for three days.

He glanced at his watch. 7.03am. If he was lucky, and if Bongo got a good run out, he'd be home by half past, which would make it... He took his notebook out of his inside coat pocket and consulted the most recent page. Ah, yes. Three days, one hour and six minutes since his last bowel movement.

He wasn't usually in the habit of tracking them, but the doctor had warned him constipation was a side-effect of cocodamol and he might want to keep an eye on it. The doctor had been right. The last one had weighed just shy of two-point-five ounces, which was at the lower end of normal. He had a feeling the next one might be in with a chance of nudging an imperial pound.

7.04 now. They were fourteen minutes into the walk, by which point they'd usually reached the stile at the bottom of the mound. Cyril estimated he was a good two minutes or so away from there. On the plus side, that meant his ankle injury had only slowed him by approximately fourteen percent. It was practically fully healed.

He watched as Bongo ran up and down the hill like a mad thing, chasing imaginary rabbits and grinning into the wind as his ears flopped behind him.

'Get that blood pumping, Bongo!' he called. The poor mutt had been going stir crazy at home for the past few days, much like Cyril himself. The divergence from their tight routine hadn't done either of them any good, but it was good to be back on the proverbial horse now, even if it was trotting fourteen percent slower than usual. He'd aim to halve that deficit tomorrow, ankle permitting. There was always a chance it'd feel worse, he supposed, but it wasn't giving him too much gip at the moment. In any case, he'd spend the rest of the day with his leg elevated while watching old re-runs of Columbo, which would reduce the chances of it swelling up.

As he daydreamed about sitting and watching Peter Falk with a big mug of cocoa, Cyril's attention was tugged by the appearance of something unusual in the undergrowth to his left, flanking the old train line.

'Odd,' he said, much as he did every time he spotted something slightly off centre. It looked like an item of clothing. A green bomber jacket, perhaps. Not a brand he recognised, though.

Bongo, as if plugged into Cyril's mind, came bounding over and began nuzzling at the jacket.

'Bongo, leave!' Cyril shouted.

Bongo ignored him, tugging at the green material until finally the weight yielded, exposing what Cyril very definitely recognised as a human arm.

46

If Jack had thought he was finally starting to pull together the pieces of the puzzle that was his life, he was wrong. Emily hadn't been in touch since his visit to Ethan's flat last night. He knew he had to give her time and space to make that decision for herself, but that didn't make it hurt any less.

He'd been informed of Damian King's death the moment he'd arrived in the office, with the news only having reached the major incident team a minute or so earlier. All they'd been told at this stage was that he'd been found in undergrowth on Mildenheath Common with two gunshot wounds to the skull. It wasn't often people managed to shoot themselves in the head twice, so this could only be considered murder. Early signs were that the murder hadn't occurred on the common, which meant there'd likely be some form of trail leading back to wherever it had occurred. His ankle tag, however, showed him as still being at home.

There'd been nothing from Professional Standards, either, on the investigation into Theo Curwood. Jack had no idea whether he was in a position to look into things himself or not now that Theo was dead, and the whole investigation was starting to look murkier and murkier. Due procedure was all well and good, but there were times like this which hadn't been anticipated when those rulebooks were drawn up.

All Jack knew was that every time he got close, he was obstructed. They'd discovered Theo was corrupt, went to visit him and found him dead. They'd started leaning more heavily on Damian King and he, too, had met the same fate. Every time they got anywhere near cracking the case, they had the carpet pulled from beneath them.

The thing that worried him most was that he was starting to realise there was only one reason why that could be happening. Whatever they did, someone was one step ahead of them. That could only mean someone knew what they had planned, what their movements would be. Someone was feeding operational information to the gang.

Jack's heart pounded in his chest as he called Wendy into his office.

'We need to have a very serious conversation,' he said, careful to make sure his voice couldn't be heard from outside the room. 'You're not going to like this. I've got a horrible sinking feeling we've got a mole on board.'

Wendy's face dropped. 'A mole?'

Jack nodded. 'I think information is getting back to McCann's lot. Stuff that could only have come from this team.'

'Jesus Christ.'

'Yeah. Tell me about it,' Jack said. He'd worked with his team for years, and trusted each of them implicitly. Even Ryan MacKenzie, the newest member of the team, had proven herself to be a team player who never bent the rules. He'd known Steve and Frank for decades, Wendy had been his right-hand woman for as long as he could remember and Debbie plodded on admirably in the background. 'The more I think about it, the more I know I'm right. That's why we've never caught McCann. This goes back years, Knight.'

'Fucking hell. Are you sure about this? I mean, it's a massive thing to come out with.'

'Oh I'm sure. Even as I say it now, I'm getting more and more sure. It's got McCann's stench all over it. The inside man. Making him untouchable. Knowing everything. He's always a step ahead. Always has been. Someone's been feeding him information for years.'

'Who?'

'That's just it. I don't know. But I'm going to find out.'

Wendy took a deep breath. 'Well let's just take a step back, shall we? We don't want to go throwing accusations around. That sort of thing could ruin someone's life. We need to stay calm about this.'

'Calm? Knight, we've seen three people killed because of this case alone. Elsie Fogg had her head caved in, Theo Curwood was left hanging from his light fitting and now Damian King's munching moss on Mildenheath Common. And that's just this case. What about all the people who've been killed over the years because they got tied up with McCann's criminal empire? All because someone — someone in this office — has been feeding him sensitive operational information, making sure he always gets away with it.'

'I just think we need to stay calm. Cool heads and all that. We need to speak to Professional Standards, without a doubt.'

Jack shook his head. 'Forget it. They've been as much use as an ashtray on a motorbike. Curwood and King would still be alive if they'd pulled their fingers out. And Chrissie...' Jack tailed off, not wanting to say any more.

'Chrissie? What about her?' Wendy said, sounding concerned.

Jack sighed. 'She was attacked.'

'What? When?'

'Last night when she left work. She's fine. Battered and bruised, but she'll be fine. Definitely targeted, though. They didn't nick her handbag or her car keys, which were in her hand. It was a message to me to back off.'

'Jesus Christ,' Wendy said, for the second time that morning.

'Yeah. So you can see why I'm a bit fucked up about all this.'

Wendy sat in silence for a few moments. 'Alright,' she said, eventually. 'I've got an idea. And I think you're going to like it.'

47

Wendy told Jack that her plan meant they'd have to be a bit more Jack Culverhouse than Wendy Knight. Doing things by the book wouldn't work anymore, and she knew they had to do things a little differently. After all, they were up against a very different force — a police officer, a detective, a friend and colleague — who knew exactly what they were doing.

When Wendy told Jack her plan, he wanted to hug her. It was brilliant. Just the sort of thing that would ruffle a few feathers, stir the pot and still allow them to get away with it.

Jack and Wendy had gone to Gary McCann's house themselves. That was unusual, as it would normally be uniformed police officers who'd go to do the pickup, but Jack wanted to see the look on McCann's face, not to mention the fact that the next part of their plan needed to be kept between them. It wasn't something either of them fancied having to explain to a uniformed PC.

They'd visited McCann's house on Meadow Hill Lane a number of times in the past. They'd even arrested McCann before, but it had never been fruitful. McCann enjoyed the cat and mouse game far too much, and was always willing to welcome the police into his house, almost as if taunting them and killing them with kindness.

The security gates were already open when they arrived, so they drove straight through, parked up at the end of the long gravel driveway and knocked on the front door.

McCann had a predictable smirk on his face when he opened the front door. 'You know, I was just thinking to myself I hadn't seen you in a while, Jack. You still at it, then?'

The pair ignored his remarks, and Jack stood aside to let Wendy do the honours.

Taking a pair of metal handcuffs from her belt and clipping them onto McCann's hands, she read him his rights and informed him he was under arrest on suspicion of conspiracy to armed robbery and murder.

'Tell me,' McCann said as they helped him into the back of Jack's car. 'Has the coffee improved since the last time I visited?'

'I'm afraid not,' Jack replied. 'If anything, it's got worse.'

'Shame. Still, I'm sure I won't be there long, so I might even give it a miss if it's all the same to you.'

'Do as you please. You know how it works as well as I do.'

'If not better,' McCann replied, smirking.

Jack pulled the car back out onto Meadow Hill Lane and headed back towards the roundabout. The quickest way into the police station was to head straight over, turn right into the town car park and cut through into the back of Mildenheath Police Station's own car park. Jack, though, turned right at the roundabout and headed towards the high street.

'Taking a shortcut, Detective Inspector?' McCann asked.

Jack ignored his deliberate attempt at getting his rank wrong, and chose not to correct him. 'Something like that. Having issues with parking at the moment. I'm afraid we're going to need to park up and walk the rest of the way.' He could feel the glare of McCann's eyes in the back of his head, and tried his best not to look in his rear view mirror. It would give the game away immediately, and in any case he knew exactly which look McCann had on his face right now.

Culverhouse parked the car and he and Wendy got out, before opening the back door and helping McCann out onto the pavement.

'What's this all about?' McCann asked.

'Parking issues,' Jack replied, shrugging. 'Sorry.'

'Parking issues my arse. What's your game?'

'Don't know what you mean, Gary. I don't do games. Come on. This way.'

The quickest and easiest way to walk from where they'd parked would have been to cut down the side of the church, back into the other side of the car park and into the police station, but Jack and Wendy had other ideas. Instead, they continued to walk down the high street and along the main shopping precinct, parading Gary McCann in his handcuffs as they headed for the main crossroads, at which point they turned left, finally in the direction of the police station.

'You're doing this on purpose, aren't you?' McCann said, almost spitting with rage.

'Doing what, Gary?' Jack replied.

'Walking me through the fucking town centre in hand-cuffs. What's it all about? Come on.'

'Sorry, still don't know what you mean. We're heading to the station, aren't we?'

'Don't treat me like a cunt, Culverhouse.'

'Stop acting like one and I'll think about it,' Jack replied, beaming a smile at a passing elderly lady, who seemed utterly bemused at the sight of a man being paraded through the streets in handcuffs. 'Sex game gone wrong,' he called to her. 'We're off to find some bolt cutters.'

Wendy tried to stifle a laugh, but failed.

A couple of minutes later they were at Mildenheath Police Station. Rather than go in through the rear car park to the custody suite, they marched McCann into the main entrance and up to the front desk.

'Sorry, love,' Jack said loudly to the woman manning it. 'Problem with the back door. Can we bring Mr Gary McCann through this way into the custody suite, please? He's been arrested.'

The woman seemed confused, but played along and let them through.

When they finally reached the custody suite, Jack told the custody sergeant what McCann had been arrested for, and mentioned they'd be looking to conduct an interview at the earliest possible opportunity.

McCann requested the presence of his lawyer, who Jack knew lived nearby. They didn't need any of the usual formalities when it came to organising an interview. They had all of the material they needed, and in any case there were things they wanted to hold back. The main objective of the exercise was complete. Shake the tree and the apples will fall.

48

Gary McCann had, as expected, been a smug fuck in his interview. His lawyer had done all of the talking, and McCann had no-commented his way through. This was pretty much what they'd thought he'd do, and it really didn't matter. He'd done his walk of shame through the town and word would have got around by now. The people involved will have heard that Gary McCann had been arrested and brought into custody, and they will have started to shit themselves. Heads would be poked above parapets, arses will have started to squeak on chairs and it would suddenly get a lot easier to spot anyone involved.

Jack had addressed the team with great pride, telling them McCann had been arrested for conspiracy to armed robbery and murder, and had watched the faces of each of his team as he passed on the information, looking for any tell-tale clues as to who might have been involved. He got nothing. But that wasn't entirely surprising, because one person was missing. Detective Constable Debbie Weston.

Jack and Wendy retired to his office after the briefing.

'You're thinking what I'm thinking, aren't you?' Wendy said as Jack sat down and rubbed the bridge of his nose with his thumb and forefinger.

'If you're thinking there's someone who's conspicuous by their absence, you'd be about right,' Jack replied.

'It's a big jump to make. We need to be sure before we do anything. And in any case, what possible motive could she have?'

'Money. Simple as that. She's had to come back to work because she was haemorrhaging cash looking after her mum down on the south coast. Don't forget she was apparently on her last legs months ago. More than that. And look at her reaction the other day when I called her out. She doesn't normally react like that. She's placid. She's never blown up like that before. It's the stress, Knight. She's not used to having to watch her back and panic about being caught. And what about all those times she's come in late or knocked off early? Fuck, I don't know why I didn't see it earlier.'

'It's hardly the sort of conclusion you'd be expected to jump to, is it? You can't blame yourself.'

'I know, but I feel so bloody stupid. She's been on the team for years, Knight. There's a reason I keep my team close to me. It's because I trust them. It's not the sort of place where you dip in and out, like Milton bloody House. If you're on my team, you're on my team. Trust. Loyalty. We're a fucking team.'

Wendy let out a sigh. 'We've got to be really sure, Jack. We don't get to mess this up. Like you said, there's a massive bond. Trust and loyalty. The second we even suspect Debbie of being involved with this, that gets destroyed forever. I think we need to wait until we pick up one of McCann's associates. They'll lead us to the bent copper. We can come up with some sort of deal. They give us the name, we make sure they get treated leniently. The bent copper's a far bigger catch for us than any of McCann's henchmen. We catch the mole, we sever the link that's let him get away with god-knows how many serious crimes over the years. And we finally get to send McCann down. For a long, long time.'

Jack was clearly pained and anguished. 'I dunno. I think I need to see it for myself. I need to know what she's doing. I don't want to hear it from some jumped-up bouncer. I need to see it with my own eyes, Knight. I've known her for years. Trusted her.'

'I get that,' Wendy said. 'But I still think it would be best to wait. The damage is done now, anyway. We need to sit back, take a bit of space. We should probably pass her name on to Professional Standards, too. They're the people who need to investigate this.'

'No chance,' Jack replied, almost before Wendy had finished speaking. 'They're not bollocksing this up again. And like I said, this is personal. She's been on my team for years. If anyone's going to catch her red-handed, it won't be Professional bloody Standards. It'll be me.'

49

Jack had been sitting outside Debbie's house for almost two hours. He was thankful for his warm coat and scarf, as he'd have drained the car's battery by now if he'd had the heater on.

He couldn't sit around too much longer. For all he knew, she might be about to bed in for the night. He didn't even know what he was looking for or expecting to find, but he knew he had to do something. The way she'd reacted to the news of Theo's death had been quite telling, in retrospect. So had the way she'd tried to warn Jack off linking McCann with the robberies. It was all so out of character, and he felt like an idiot for not spotting it earlier.

He felt convinced the motive must have been money. Her mum was still refusing to die and eating up cash in care home fees. He'd overheard her mentioning to Ryan that it was costing seven hundred pounds a week. At that level, she'd be virtually bankrupting herself. Even her DC's salary wouldn't keep her afloat. There was every chance McCann had got wind of this and pounced. He was an expert at spotting desperation. Jack hoped that was the case, anyway. He prayed she'd just had her head turned by money. That would be foolish of her. Still completely unforgivable, but marginally better than finding out she was outright corrupt.

He just wished she could have said something to him. He couldn't have helped much. Not really. Not to the tune of seven hundred quid a week. But he could have at least listened. There must have been something they could have done.

But the tree had been shaken now. McCann had been arrested and paraded through the streets. There was one more thing he could do, though. It'd be kill or cure, but it would be well worth it either way.

He typed out a text message on his phone and sent it to Debbie, his heart skipping a beat as he pressed the *Send* button.

Just thought you might like to know we arrested McCann today. New evidence came to light earlier. Got him bang to rights. Might finally be the one that brings him down!

. . .

He locked his phone and put it back on the passenger seat next to him. He didn't want the screen lighting up his face, lest a passer-by spotted him sitting out here in his car.

He gave it a minute or so, then looked back at the screen. It was showing that Debbie had read the message, but she hadn't replied and wasn't currently composing a reply.

Jack stared at the screen, willing her to say something. The silence was deafening, and a lack of instinctive response really wasn't helping her case at all.

A couple of minutes later, still clutching the phone in the hope of Debbie saying something — anything — he noticed movement. Her living room light went out, and a few seconds later her front door opened and she stepped out, closing and locking it behind her before heading for her car.

She seemed to be in a hurry, but Jack told himself that was probably just the cold. No-one would have wanted to be outside for long in this. He watched as she started the car, pulled out onto the road and headed away from him.

He started his own car, glad she'd not driven past him, and drove in the same direction, keeping enough distance but at the same time careful not to lose her. He was pleased it was dark, as that'd make it difficult for her to see the make or model of car behind her in the dazzle of his headlights. He'd have to be careful not to get stuck behind her at a set of lights, though.

As he followed Debbie down Hill Road, he stopped

and flashed his lights to let another motorist out of a side street. That would put another car between him and Debbie, which would reduce the chances of her spotting him. He just hoped the doddery old bugger would keep up a decent speed so he didn't end up losing her.

A few minutes later, Debbie's car pulled over to the side of the road in a smart residential estate. The houses were all detached — probably four bedrooms each, Jack estimated. He stopped his car a little further up the road and tried to think if there was anyone they were aware of who lived round here, but no-one came to mind.

His phone vibrated in his pocket, and he glanced at the screen. It was a reply from Debbie.

Great news! See u tomorrow.

He looked up again and watched as she got out of her car, pulled her coat closed against the icy wind and half walked, half jogged over the road and up a driveway.

There was no way he'd be able to see who owned the house if he didn't get closer, so he pulled back out onto the road and drove slowly towards the house, stopping right outside, but on the other side of the road. If Debbie looked behind her, she'd see him, but there was no going back now. He had to see this for himself.

His heart thumped in his chest as he watched her ring the doorbell and wait for someone to come to the door.

Eventually, he saw the door begin to open, revealing a man a few inches taller than Debbie, who looked familiar. It took Jack a second to place him, but then Jack realised why. He was far more used to seeing him in the Prince Albert, the pub next door to the police station where the team occasionally enjoyed after-work drinks. The man was Roy, the landlord.

'You cheeky bugger,' Jack murmured to himself, as he watched them embrace and kiss, before going inside and closing the door behind them.

Roy was married to Linda, and the pair mostly lived in the flat above the pub, although they'd kept their family home too. They had grown-up children who'd long flown the nest, and the pub was supposed to be a fun experiment for their early retirement.

Jack shook his head and chuckled to himself. That was why Debbie had been so on edge and acting out of sorts recently. She was seeing a married man. He supposed she needed to get her kicks somewhere after spending all her time looking after her dying mum, but he certainly hadn't expected this. She'd been single and unattached for as long as he'd known her, and presumed she'd never had a partner in her life. She'd certainly never spoken about one. Now he knew why.

It still didn't mean Debbie wasn't the one in league with McCann, but things were starting to make sense to Jack now. Deep down, he knew it wasn't Debbie. Couldn't be Debbie. He felt like an idiot for even thinking it.

He picked up his phone and called Wendy.

'I've got an apology to make. Two, actually,' he said when she answered. 'I didn't listen to your advice. I followed Debbie tonight, to see where she went. I won't go into details, but let's just say I don't think she's our mole.'

Wendy went silent for a moment before speaking. 'Yeah. I was just about to call you, actually. I didn't listen to my own advice, either. I stayed at the office and went back and did a bit more digging. I've found something. And I don't think you're going to like it.'

50

Jack swung his car into the parking space and let himself into the staff entrance of Mildenheath Police Station. He jogged up the stairs to the major incident room and walked into the office.

'Go on. Hit me with it,' he said, sitting down next to Wendy. She hadn't told him any details on the phone, and had instead insisted he might want to come in and see it for himself. Besides which, it would mean she might be able to stop him flying off the handle again.

'I've been going back through the files and trying to work out where we might have been derailed,' Wendy said. 'Things started to go wrong pretty near the start. I've not gone through much of the rest of things, but I don't think I need to. Don't think I want to, either.'

'Get to the point,' Jack said, gritting his teeth. He didn't want to hear it either, didn't want to be told someone on his team was a mole, but he needed to know who it was, and needed to see the evidence that proved it.

'I started by looking at the local CCTV we had access to. The request went in for all the usual data protection stuff to the council and a few local businesses. All came back fine, nothing missed there. So I went back and looked through it to see if anything had been missed on the footage itself. The BMW that was associated with the petrol station robberies appears on three different cameras. Pretty clear views, too. The plates are fake — I've already checked that.'

'This wasn't on any of the notes, was it?' Jack said.

'No. When the CCTV was inspected as part of the investigation, the notes say there was nothing of interest and that the BMW couldn't be seen or identified.'

His heart began to sink. He already knew the answer to the question, but he had to ask it. 'Who inspected the CCTV? Who left that note?' he said.

Wendy looked him in the eyes, her own starting to well up. 'Frank.'

51

Jack sat with his head in his hands. Frank Vine had been one of his closest colleagues for as long as he could remember. The man had been flirting with the idea of retirement for a couple of years now, and had given Jack the best part of two decades' service. Although he was lazy and largely just seeing out the days until he could pick up his pension, there was no way in a million years he would have ever suspected him of being a mole.

He was gutted. Torn apart. When he thought about it, he realised the betrayal must have gone back years. How long had Frank been feeding McCann information, making sure he always stayed at arm's length from their investigations. Was that why he'd always managed to get off? Was that why the evidence was always just slightly too weak? Jack had clearly underestimated Frank for years.

'I need to speak to him,' he said, standing up, but finding Wendy's hand grabbing his wrist.

'No. You can't. We've got what we need. There'll be more. We need to take this to Professional Standards. This goes way above our pay grade, Jack.'

He shook her off. 'It's not about pay grades. It's about loyalty. It's about betrayal. He's betrayed me, Knight. He's betrayed us all.'

Wendy could hear his voice starting to break. 'I know. But take a minute. Please. We can't rush into things.'

Jack looked at her, the tears welling in his eyes. 'Do me a favour, Knight. Just one thing.'

'What?'

'Let me speak to him.'

'Why? What are you going to do?'

'I don't know. I don't know. Maybe I can get him to spill the beans on McCann. I'll make a deal with him. He tells me everything, gives me enough to send McCann down for the rest of his life, and I'll make sure Frank gets an easy ride. We can pension him off. He'll be gone.'

'No, Jack. That's not right. If we give this to Professional Standards, they'll see Frank gets what he deserves and it'll be more than enough to send McCann down too.'

Jack shook his head. 'I can't risk that. I know Frank. I know him better than anybody. I can push the right buttons. I *need* this rub on McCann, Knight. You have no idea. No bloody idea. That man has made it his mission to terrorise me and frustrate everything I do for the last thirty-five years. Do you know, I still see his spotty, arrogant little teenage face, sneering at me. It was my first week in CID. I nabbed him for burglary. It was the first time I ever came across him, and I knew right away it wasn't going to be the last. I could see the look in his eyes. He had his prey. He was locked on. I know you lot think it's always been me going after him, but you're wrong. All I've been doing is trying, desperately fucking trying, to get my one shot at outdoing him. I've hung in here all these years, just waiting for him to slip up. Waiting for that fucker to get a charge from the CPS. Waiting to see him disappear out of that courtroom and back down into the cells. And there is no way — no way — I am giving up that chance now. We're so close.'

Wendy could see how much this was eating Jack up from the inside. 'I know. I know what this means to you. And I know how much Frank has betrayed you, betrayed all of us. But you can use this to get into Professional Standards' good books. If you make a deal with Frank or get involved yourself, it'll look worse for you. There's a chance they'll throw the case out entirely. It's got to be kept clean, or there's no way you'll get that day in court. We can't muck it up now. Like you said, we're so close.'

'I dunno..'

'Think about it. This is your chance to do things the right way. It'll shut Penny Andrews up, too. There's no way she can carry on with her restructuring if you're the one who's rooted out corruption in the force before her own senior officers even got wind of it. Now imagine what she'll do if she finds out you interfered in that. It'll be curtains for all of us, Jack. Frank might have betrayed you, but we haven't. We've all stayed loyal. We've stuck together. And we're not about to change that now.'

Jack looked at Wendy. He was desperate to have just five minutes in a room with Frank, but deep down he knew Wendy was right.

He looked down at the floor, swallowed hard, then looked back up at her. 'We need more people like you at the top, Knight. Seriously.'

52

Over the years, Frank and his wife had got used to eating their evening meal just before going to bed. When he ended up working late, she'd originally left his portion in the microwave for him, but had gradually decided to wait up for him so they could eat together. Since she'd been disabled, Frank had usually been the one to rustle up the meals in any case.

Still, there wasn't long left now. Frank had finally made the decision to retire, and would tell Jack at some point this week. They'd done the sums and realised they'd be pretty comfortable, especially if they managed to relocate.

'I'm coming round to the idea of Cornwall myself,' he said.

'Too expensive,' his wife replied. 'Too many people buying second homes. We wouldn't be left with much after selling this place and buying down there.'

'I think we'll be alright,' Frank replied, smiling. 'We've got some tucked away in some savings accounts. We'll go through it all tomorrow.'

Frank had always been the one to handle their finances. That was something he'd been grateful for recently. They'd been talking about relocating in retirement for years — almost as long as Frank had been talking about retirement — and they'd been split between Cornwall and the Lake District. Both had their pros and cons, but Frank's reasoning had been that Cornwall would have better weather and a slower pace of life. Besides which, there were only certain areas of the county that took the tourist influx throughout the summer, whereas the Lake District was mobbed all over, all year round.

'A guy I went to school with moved down there a year or so ago,' Frank said. 'Saw it pop up on Facebook. Right out in the middle of nowhere. Surrounded by fields, they are. No traffic, no crime, no nothing. Totally different pace of life. Beautiful place to retire.'

His wife raised her eyebrows in a way which told him she completely agreed that Cornwall would be a lovely place to move to, but she hadn't given up on the dream of the Lake District just yet.

Frank's mobile phone buzzed in his pocket. Just twice, which told him it was a text message. He took the phone out of his pocket and looked at the screen. It was a text message from Jack Culverhouse. He didn't unlock his phone to read the full message. He didn't need to. The first few words of the message preview told him all he needed to know. All of a sudden, he wasn't very hungry any more.

'Frank? What is it?' his wife asked, noticing he'd turned pale.

Frank swallowed, his throat dry. 'Nothing. Nothing.' The sounds of the sirens in the distance gradually grew louder, until the only thing drowning them out was the pounding of the blood in his own eardrums. 'I'm sorry,' he croaked. 'I'm so sorry.'

'What for? Frank? What's wrong?'

Frank swallowed again, then slowly pushed his chair back and stood up, his face reflecting the familiar glow of the flashing police lights as they heard the knock at the door.

53

One week later.

Jack tried to steady his breathing as the officer led him down the corridor towards Frank's cell. He had to keep calm.

He'd rehearsed what he wanted to say a thousand times or more in his own head, but he knew he'd likely scrap the lot when he got in there. After all, what could possibly be said?

He hadn't come face to face with Frank since he was arrested. It had probably been for the best. Professional Standards had been involved, even though Jack had retained some control by authorising Frank's arrest. He was confident the rot went no further, and that the most pressing matter was to ensure that Frank was taken in before McCann panicked and got to him first. McCann had been re-arrested at the same time by other officers, and had been subsequently charged and released on bail awaiting a court date. This had been necessary to ensure McCann couldn't skip the country or go into hiding. This way, they'd have far more power to pursue him if he attempted it. With Frank having been taken in, word will have got back to McCann very quickly. Frank, on the other hand, had been kept in a cell at a different police station outside of the county, mainly to ensure his own safety before his trial.

The officer opened the door to the cell and let Jack in. Frank didn't seem entirely surprised to see him. Perhaps it had only been a matter of time.

'Jack. I don't know what to say,' Frank said, standing up.

Jack nodded. 'I don't know what I want you to say.'

'I'm sorry,' Frank said, eventually. The words didn't even begin to scratch the surface, though.

'I need to know why, Frank.'

Frank sat back down on the hard plastic monstrosity he called a bed, and sighed. 'Where do I start?'

'At the beginning,' Jack said, his voice devoid of emotion.

'I don't really know where it started. When my missus got ill, I suppose. I got talking to a bloke in the pub one night. He'd clocked what I did and who I was. Thinking back now I reckon he knew anyway. It was a setup job. It was meant to be a one-off. An easy payday that'd pay for her treatment and give me a nice retirement. Nothing heavy. Not a case we were on, so I wasn't the only one who got approached, I can tell you that,' Frank said, as if that was any excuse.

'Don't look at me for sympathy,' Jack said. 'You might not be the only one they approached, but you were the one thick enough to fall for it.'

Frank stayed silent.

'Tell me something. I need to know. Were you anything to do with what happened to Chrissie?' Jack desperately hoped the answer was "no", because he couldn't possibly account for his reaction otherwise.

Frank shook his head. 'It was all McCann. Honestly. It wasn't meant to escalate. I didn't want it to. I was in over my head. But after the old woman died it all went tits up and McCann wanted to send a warning to you to make you back off. He was in over his head and so was I. We all were.'

'So you were involved,' Jack said, his voice gravelly as he tried to hold himself back from kicking Frank's head in.

'No. Honestly. I wasn't. McCann wanted to go for your girl, Jack. He wanted it to be Emily, but I managed to convince him not to do it. I couldn't have him doing that to her.'

Jack wanted to deck him, but managed to find enough restraint to stop himself. 'You'll testify against him, won't you?' he finally said. He could tell from Frank's body language the answer wasn't as straightforward as he'd hoped.

'I dunno. I don't think I can. I can't. If I do, I'll lose

everything. He'll go for the missus. He'll burn the house down. Fuck knows what he'll do, Jack. He's a right nasty piece of work.'

'Oh, I know, Frank. I know. Why do you think I've been trying to send the fucker down for the past thirty-five years? Only something, some*one* kept getting in the way of that, didn't they?'

Frank shook his head in despair. 'Jack, you really don't get it. That's not what happened. You need to believe me.'

'Believe you?' Jack spat. 'Don't make me laugh. Do you have any idea how much I'd love — *love* — to dive over there right now and smash your head off that wall? Because I'll tell you. It's a lot. But I'm not. I'm standing here, keeping myself calm, telling you we can protect you. We can protect your wife. We can shield you from McCann. You can relocate. A new life. A new identity.'

'Oh Jack. I wish I could take you up on that. I really do. You seriously have no idea what you're dealing with here, do you? McCann has people everywhere. He can get to anyone he likes, anywhere he likes. He's got more than the odd copper in his pocket, you know.'

Jack ignored his comments. 'I'm giving you a chance to redeem yourself here, Frank. One final chance. After this, there's no more. McCann isn't on your side. You can't protect him. He won't be protecting you any more. He'll only look after you and your missus for as long as you're useful to him. That ship's sailed. You'll both be finished. I'm not looking at the past few weeks. I'm looking at the past few years. You might have betrayed me, Frank. Might have betrayed the entire team. Betrayed your family. Betrayed yourself. But I'm a bigger man than that. The only person who can make sure you're looked after — properly looked after — is me.' Jack stepped forward. 'Now I'm going to ask you one last time to testify against McCann and at least do the dignified thing. For yourself. For your family.'

Frank looked at Jack with misted eyes, his body shaking. Slowly, he shook his head. 'I can't, Jack. I can't.'

54

The job tended to bring a lot of drama and events which resulted in the need to clear one's head at the best of times, but the last week or so had thrown up some of the most difficult realisations Wendy had ever had to deal with.

She knew Mildenheath CID would never be the same again. It couldn't be. It would be forever tainted by Frank's actions, by what he did. Once the dust had settled, the new dynamics would become clear. It might be that the action would finally move to Milton House. In any case, Wendy knew this was the beginning of a new chapter, and a turning point in her career that she'd never forget.

After all of the drama and the highs and lows, she was glad to be spending the evening with her feet up in front of the telly with Xav.

She'd been doing a lot of thinking over the past week or so. Events had put a very different shine on things, and she'd begun to realise — more than ever — what this job meant to people. She looked at Frank Vine, having spent the vast majority of his career as a DS, comfortable in his job, never really pushing himself. He'd got stale, looking forward only to retirement. And when that time had almost come, his boredom had led him off track and his entire career had been thrown away, as if it had never happened. He'd left disgraced, without a police pension and with every little good thing he did completely wiped out by one stupid move.

'I've been having a think,' she said to Xav, who seemed to be on the verge of drifting off to sleep as the bright light of the television danced across his face in the relative darkness.

'Mmmm?'

'I know I've said this before, but I mean it this time. I'm going to take the exam. I'm going for the promotion.'

Xav turned his head and smiled, before reaching his arm across and holding her hand. 'That's brilliant news. Seriously. You're going to be amazing.'

Wendy smiled back. 'I just think there's a lot that needs doing. Mildenheath's special, but if good people don't step up to keep it that way, that might not always be the case. I want to help improve things, and that needs me to take a step up. I don't want everything everyone has fought for over the years to be taken away from us because I didn't have the guts to stand up. Jack's spent his career defending this unit, and not just for himself. For all of us, and everyone who went before him. People like Dad.'

Xav squeezed her hand. 'I'm proud of you, you know. Listen,' he said, shuffling awkwardly in his seat. 'There's something I've been meaning to tell you. I left it a few days because of everything you had going on, but I think now's the right time to tell you. I've had an offer on my house.'

'Seriously?' Wendy asked. She'd been certain he'd been doing the bare minimum to get his house sold, sure that he was hanging on to his last shred of independence as an excuse not to commit fully to her.

'Yeah. A bit below asking price, but I think it's fair. I told them I'd think about it, speak to you.'

'It's not my house, Xav. I can't make that decision for you.'

'Oh, I know. I wasn't asking you to. I know what I'm going to do. I'm going to accept the offer.'

Wendy smiled again. This would finally mean Xav would move in with her, or that they could eventually put her house on the market too and pool their money together to buy a bigger place of their own. If she had an Inspector's salary to throw into the mix as well, and if Xav managed to achieve his dream of becoming a specialist officer rather than civilian support staff... This might just be the fresh start they both needed.

'I'm sorry it took me so long,' he said. 'I've got to be honest, I was a bit worried for a while. I just thought, once the place is gone that's it. No getting it back. It's been my home for years, and I kind of felt as if I was intruding on yours. As if I'd always feel like the lodger. And if it doesn't work, I'd be out on my arse with nothing. I guess I just didn't want to risk getting hurt again, but then I watched you going into work every morning, always with that risk of losing everything, and I asked myself what the hell I was doing. Why was I so attached to a pile of bricks and plaster? Memories, I suppose. But we can always build new memories.'

She'd never heard Xav open up quite like this before. He'd usually been more quiet and reserved. She knew he'd had difficulties in the past and had been hurt, but he'd never been keen to tell her much about it. Perhaps they'd both changed. Perhaps they were both at the beginning of a new era. Perhaps they were both ready to move forward.

55

The next morning, Jack found himself surprisingly pleased to have been called into the Chief Constable's office for a meeting with Hawes and Penny Andrews, the county's Police and Crime Commissioner. It was an event he'd usually have dreaded, but not now.

The atmosphere in the team had been sour ever since word had got out about Frank's arrest and everything that had gone before it. There was a horrible air of not knowing who to trust, and whether the rot had gone any further. Even if it hadn't, everyone felt betrayed by Frank, a man they'd seen as a friend and trusted colleague for many years. All of their efforts had been tainted, and the work they'd done over the years had been largely fruitless, not through their own efforts but because of one of their own thinking he could make a quick buck on the side at their expense.

Jack had done his best to try to raise morale, but that

had been almost impossible. He'd been more seriously affected than any of them, having taken Frank under his wing and relied on him as one of his steadiest Detective Sergeants. The fact that Frank had taken the money rather than coming to Jack and helping him use it to nail McCann once and for all had cut deep.

Part of him was looking forward to seeing Mildenheath CID wound up. He didn't know if there was any coming back from this. It wasn't the way he wanted things to end, but it might be easier than trying to fight the inevitable. In any case, he couldn't be held responsible for what had happened. There was only one man who could claim that accolade.

When Jack entered the Chief Constable's office, he could see that Charles Hawes had been knocked sideways by recent events, too. The man was ashen-faced, although that wasn't entirely unusual when in the presence of Penny Andrews.

'Jack, thank you for joining us,' Andrews said, a smug look on her face.

Jack wondered what possible pleasure she could derive from discovering that one of her officers had been corrupt. This was not the sort of situation for political point scoring, and it demonstrated to Jack exactly why politics and policing should never mix.

'I realise recent events will have been quite distressing,' she said. 'I know you have a close-knit team, and the discovery of what had been going on under your nose must have hurt. It's shocked all of us, and it's made me realise more than ever that we might need to change a few processes and aspects of the organisational structure in order to ensure integrity and public trust in the police service.'

'Listen,' Jack said, not in the mood for any nonsense or corporate buzzwords. 'Just get on with it, alright? If you're here to shut us down, make it quick instead of beating around the bush and boring the shit out of me, will you?'

Andrews looked at him, evidently not quite sure what to say. 'Uh, no. That isn't what I've come here for,' she said. 'Quite the opposite, in fact. I've heard nothing but good things about your team. I know you're not keen on me, and just think I'm a career politician, but you couldn't be further from the truth. I care passionately about policing. If I'm going to make the most of my new position, I need the right people around me. I'm offering you the opportunity to work for me, Jack.'

Jack looked first at Hawes, then back at Andrews. 'Work for you?'

'With me. Work with me,' Andrews said, correcting herself. 'I'm keen that my position isn't seen as solely political, and I'm looking to bring a couple of senior police officers on board as advisors, to ensure we're all singing from the same hymn sheet.'

Jack was pretty sure he and Andrews would never be singing from the same hymn sheet for as long as they lived, but he decided to humour her for a bit.

'And what exactly would this role entail?' he asked, catching Hawes's eye and seeing no emotion on the man's face.

'It's largely advisory, but well remunerated. It's ideal for a senior officer with a record of long and distinguished service, who may be approaching the end of his career.'

Jack caught Hawes's eye again, and this time he thought he detected a glimmer of something — some life and some spark that had returned. Hawes must know that was the sort of comment that would rile Jack. Even though he'd realised himself he wouldn't be far off retirement, the last thing he needed was to hear it from Penny bloody Andrews.

'I see,' he replied. 'And how would that affect the structure of the team here?'

'Well, obviously you wouldn't remain in your existing role. We might be able to work something out on that front, though. It's all flexible.'

'What I mean is, is Mildenheath CID safe?'

'Of course. I have no intention to make any changes to the organisation at this stage. The unit will remain as it always has been for the foreseeable future.'

'And that's a cast-iron guarantee? Regardless of my decision, Mildenheath CID stays as is?'

'Correct,' Andrews said, smiling.

Jack looked at Hawes, then back at Penny Andrews. 'I see. In that case, I think it's a pretty easy decision to make. A no-brainer, in fact.'

Penny Andrews beamed from ear to ear. 'That's wonderful news, Jack. I'm so looking forward to working with you.'

'Oh no,' Jack said. 'Sorry, I think there might have been some misunderstanding. I won't be taking you up on your offer.'

Penny Andrews's face dropped. 'Sorry? Why on earth not?'

'Honestly? Because I think you're the worst kind of spineless career politician, using the police force as a stepping stone to your ultimate payday of becoming an MP. You don't give two shits about anyone other than yourself or furthering your own career and public image. You enjoy trampling over people you see as subordinate to you, you get a kick out of the drama of internal police politics rather than wanting to settle them, and I personally couldn't think of anything worse than having to spend a second more in your company than I need to. I could probably go on, but I think that just about covers it.'

Charles Hawes's eyes were alight, either with shock at what Jack had just done, or schoolboy excitement at his friend having just stood up to the headmistress.

'I see,' Andrews said, clearly chastened but keen not to let it show. 'So I presume I should take that as a "no"?'

'I'd use a few more words than that, personally, but that's about the gist of it,' Jack replied.

Penny Andrews shoved her tongue into the inside of her cheek and nodded. 'Right. Well, thank you for your

time, Detective Chief Inspector. Chief Constable. I'll see
myself out.'

Neither man dared look at Andrews. It was unavoidable that this would come back to bite them both on the arse
in one way or another in the future, but for now both were
very much enjoying watching Penny Andrews walk away
with her tail between her legs.

56

Three weeks later.

Gary McCann stepped out through the bi-fold doors, into his back garden and took a deep lungful of the crisp morning air. It was a good time to be alive.

It was always a good time to be alive, and he particularly enjoyed this time of the morning. Regardless of the time of year, he always came out here first thing and stood with a cup of tea, watching nature wake up in front of him.

A small nagging voice had, for a short while, told him he might not have too many of these mornings left, but it had quietened down in the last few days. Everything would be taken care of. It always was.

He knew the police would be busily trying to gather

their evidence while he was on bail, awaiting a court date. He also knew it didn't matter what they came up with — he was always at least three steps ahead of them.

He loved the English court system, which meant the burden of proof was always on the prosecution, and that the jury had to be left without any reasonable doubt that the defendant was guilty. That watermark was beautiful, and Gary had borne it in mind his whole life. As long as plenty of reasonable doubt could always be introduced, he was home and dry. Introducing reasonable doubt had become one of his most successful business models.

His brief thought they were in with a decent chance, too. It wasn't often Gary McCann had found himself in a court of law, but the prospect didn't scare him. After all, it was just another risk that came with the job. He knew how to play the game better than anyone else, and he didn't have to stick to the same rules and procedure as the police. Their hands were tied. The burden of proof was on them. It was like throwing stones at a dog tied to a lamp post. It could bark and yap all it liked; it wasn't getting anywhere near him unless he walked in the wrong direction.

Word had got back to him that Frank Vine was starting to waver. That wasn't an issue. Not in the long-term. That could be dealt with. Gary didn't worry that Frank might take the stand and testify against him, finally developing a conscience after so long. It wouldn't get to that. The whole issue would be nipped in the bud pretty quickly. He only had to give the word.

Too many men of his stature ruled with an iron fist. The problem with that was it was short-sighted. When the shit hit the fan and they got arrested and charged, there was no end of people willing to come forward to testify. He'd seen it many times himself over the years. He, on the other hand, had a string of local business owners who'd be only too pleased to help him out in return, especially after he'd saved their livelihoods and families. To them, Gary McCann was an angel.

He watched as a pigeon landed on his vast lawn and started to peck at the hard ground. The small summer birds had long since disappeared, but they'd be back once the weather warmed up. Personally, Gary enjoyed the winter mornings. He liked watching the rising sun glistening off the frost, feeling the slight burn in his lungs as he took in that first deep, cold breath.

In the quiet of the crisp Mildenheath morning, he thought he heard the distant sound of footsteps on gravel. He knew straight away what it was, but there wasn't much point in doing anything about it. It was all part of the process. Nothing new, although they were usually a little lighter-handed than this.

He leaned back against the house and took in another deep breath of air as he heard, then saw, two men appear in the garden, having scaled the back gate.

'Morning, officers,' he said, over the sound of them telling him to turn around and face the wall. He raised his hands in the air and smiled. He'd had a fair idea this was coming at some point. It was all part of the game. He didn't mind. He was protected. If they thought a lowly Detective Sergeant was the height of Gary McCann's influence, they were gravely mistaken.

57

Frank stared at the floor of his cell, shaking. He still couldn't quite come to terms with the fact he'd been kept in here for so long. It was for his own protection, they told him. There was no way in hell this was safer than being allowed to stay at home. Even Gary fucking McCann had been released on bail. Where was the justice in that?

Frank knew he'd been thrown under the bus. Yes, he got a slightly comfier bed and a couple of small luxuries other prisoners didn't get, but these were only holding cells. They weren't meant to house anyone for more than twenty-hour hours, never mind the best part of a month.

It was an odd atmosphere. The officers who worked here clearly knew what he was in for. Word will have got around quickly. He could tell by the looks on some of their faces exactly what they thought of him. To most serving police officers, a corrupt officer was worse than a career criminal.

He didn't know how he was going to fare in proper prison. Police officers didn't tend to do all that well, for obvious reasons. He doubted if he'd be given his own area somewhere, away from danger. There'd always be danger. There was no getting out of it now.

His solicitor reckoned he could get a reduced sentence — perhaps even a suspended one, at a push — if they could convince the jury Frank had been coerced by McCann while in a vulnerable position. His long record of service would help too, but not much. Either way, life had changed irrevocably. Even the minuscule possibility of being completely absolved wouldn't help all that much. McCann would still be furious, and Frank would always have a target painted on his back. He'd lost his friends, his colleagues. He'd certainly lost his pride. In many ways, prison would be a safer option.

He jumped as the sound of the cell door unlocking rattled around the cold, concrete room.

A pair of feet came into view, and he looked up to see the police officer handing him a plate of food.

'Pork in black bean sauce, tonight. And a bread roll. I've cut it in half for you,' the officer said, looking pointedly at him.

Frank swallowed, took the tray and put it on his lap. He looked at the bread roll and lifted the top off, seeing a glistening steel razor blade nestled comfortably in the fluffy bread, complete with makeshift wooden handle.

Frank started to tremble harder. Visions of everything he'd achieved, everything he'd lost, came before him. He thought of his wife, of his family. What did it matter? It was all lost now. All gone. All through his own greed, selfishness and stupidity. What did a lifetime of hard graft and good honour count in the face of one daft decision? That wasn't the way the world worked. It wasn't a points-based system. People only ever remember the bad things.

'Trust me,' the officer said, leaning forward and whispering. 'It's easier if you do it yourself.'

Frank looked at the razor blade and started to cry. The main thing was his wife was going to be okay. He knew Jack would see to that. The guvnor would be angry for a while, but he was a good man. He'd see to it that everything was alright. He knew he would.

58

Jack hoovered his living room floor for the third time that day. It wasn't a job he had ever been keen on before — he got the vacuum cleaner out perhaps once a fortnight, if that — but he'd had enough of sitting around the house moping.

Moping meant thinking, and he'd had enough of thinking. Nothing good ever came of it. All he did was brood about the situation with Emily, what Frank had done and which direction his life was going to take. Telling Penny Andrews to go fuck herself had been a brief moment of delight, but in everything else he was very much still waiting for the dust to settle. Retirement, however, was very much at the forefront of his mind.

Chrissie had already gone up to bed. She was still on strong painkillers for her leg, and Jack had moved her in with him until she'd recovered. She was able to get around on crutches much better now, and she'd taken to sleeping upstairs again on the doctors' advice. Jack was pleased to have finally put the camp bed away and made his living room a living room again, rather than a makeshift bedroom. He didn't mind, though. Looking after her had given him something to do. She'd told him time and time again she wasn't an invalid and was perfectly capable of getting around on crutches, but he'd needed something to take his mind off everything else. Deep down, he knew she knew that.

He unplugged the vacuum cleaner and tied the cord around it, before putting it back in the cupboard under the stairs. As he did so, he heard the sound of the front door unlocking and opening. There was only one other person who had a key, and Jack knew immediately who it was.

He also knew he couldn't panic or react too much. This had to be normal. It had to be undramatic, yet welcoming.

'Em,' he said, smiling as he watched her walk into the living room. 'Sorry, just doing a bit of hoovering.'

Emily flicked her eyebrows briefly upwards. 'Well, you were right. You have changed.'

Jack let out a small chuckle. 'It's good to see you,' he said. As he stepped towards her, he could see she'd been crying. 'Everything okay?'

'Not really. Ethan and I had an argument.'

'Oh,' Jack replied, keen not to overreact or jump to the conclusion that it had all been Ethan's fault. 'Do you want to talk about it?'

'No, not really.'

'That's fine,' Jack said, wanting to kick Ethan Turner's head in. 'I'm here if you want to, though. Are you... staying?'

Emily shrugged. 'Well it's my home, isn't it?'

Jack smiled. 'Of course it is. It's always your home. You know I love having you here. And I really am sorry about what happened before. I won't go on about it, but I just wanted you to know that.'

'It's fine.'

'Seriously, Em. Whatever you need, I'll be here to support you. We're a family,' he said, looking down at her belly. 'All of us.' Noticing that Emily was on the verge of tears again, he pulled her into a hug, which was only broken by the sound of Chrissie trying to get down the stairs on her crutches. 'Woah, hang on. Let me give you a hand,' he said.

'I'm not a cripple, Jack. I can manage. Hi, Emily. I thought it might be you. How've you been?'

'Yeah, alright. Not as good as you, by the looks of things.'

'I'll heal. Much better than I was, anyway.'

'I heard what happened. At school. Everyone's talking about it.'

Chrissie exchanged an awkward look with Jack. 'Yes, well, it's nice to be popular, I suppose.'

'Do you want something to eat?' Jack asked Emily.

'It's cool. I'll do myself a jacket potato,' his daughter replied, chucking her bag down next to the sofa and making her way through to the kitchen.

'Like she's never been away,' Chrissie said, hobbling across the room and sitting down on the sofa.

'Shouldn't you be in bed?' Jack asked.

'Couldn't sleep. Thought I'd come down and see Emily. And you, of course.'

'Of course,' Jack replied, smiling. Chrissie's sleep patterns had been a little abnormal thanks to the strong painkillers, just as his had been thanks to his stress levels, and it was amazing how often the two bizarre schedules seemed to match up.

'Is she back?' Chrissie mouthed, thumbing a gesture towards the kitchen.

'Dunno,' Jack said. 'I hope so.'

'Maybe things are looking up.'

Jack had thought that many times himself over the years, but had usually been proved wrong. This time, though, he hoped Chrissie was right. 'Maybe,' he said, sitting down next to her. 'Listen, there's something I wanted to tell you.'

'Go on.'

'I haven't been entirely honest with you. I mean, I really love having you here, and I love spending time with you and I'm really excited by where things are going with us.'

'Was that you being dishonest?' Chrissie said, smiling.

'No, that part's a bit more... delicate. Helen and I aren't actually divorced. We're separated. The divorce bit is tricky, because she doesn't have a fixed address and keeps disappearing. If truth be told, I don't even know which country she's in right now.'

Chrissie looked at him and smiled. 'Is that it?'

'Well, yeah. I'd have thought it was a pretty big thing.'

'It's fine, honestly. I understand. I'm happy just being with you. Although I must admit, I'm a bit annoyed that she might end up getting hold of the stuff I'd had my eye on.'

Jack laughed, for the first time in a long time. Perhaps retirement, when it came, wouldn't be so bad.

ACKNOWLEDGMENTS

Although writing in an established series does undoubtedly make things a little easier, this book — as all books do — owes a great deal to many people. Although not financially, of course, because that would be silly.

My thanks as always go to Graham Bartlett for his experience and expertise at the highest levels of policing. Information on Professional Standards, covert policing and other aspects are notoriously difficult to come by, but Graham is always unfailingly generous with his time and advice. Any places in which I've strayed from realistic police procedure are entirely my responsibility. Realism is a key aim for me, but story must win out.

Thank you again to my small team of early readers (by which I mean my wife and my mum) who managed to pick out the most embarrassing errors before the manuscript left the building. To Lucy, for her dedication and enthusiasm for my books, and for having been such a wonderful and forthright editor over the years. My books would be noticeably poorer were it not for her input.

For this book, my biggest debt of gratitude must go to Mark Boutros. This man is nothing short of a genius when it comes to storytelling, and he's helped me out of Plot Hole Hell on a number of occasions. Between us, we managed to get from a few thousand scrappy words and a vague idea of plot direction to a finished novel within the space of three weeks. Not only that, but I'm eternally grateful for his patience and enthusiasm for dealing with endless phone calls and text messages to tell him I've buggered the plot up and need rescuing. Even after eleven years writing this series, I still run into roadblocks and difficulties more often than most people might think.

And, of course, my greatest and final thanks go to you, the readers. Your love for Jack and Wendy and the rest of the team is what keeps me going.

MORE BOOKS BY ADAM CROFT

RUTLAND CRIME SERIES

1. What Lies Beneath
2. On Borrowed Time
3. In Cold Blood

KNIGHT & CULVERHOUSE CRIME THRILLERS

1. Too Close for Comfort
2. Guilty as Sin
3. Jack Be Nimble
4. Rough Justice
5. In Too Deep
6. In The Name of the Father
7. With A Vengeance
8. Dead & Buried
9. In Too Deep
10. Snakes & Ladders

PSYCHOLOGICAL THRILLERS

- Her Last Tomorrow

- Only The Truth
- In Her Image
- Tell Me I'm Wrong
- The Perfect Lie
- Closer To You

KEMPSTON HARDWICK MYSTERIES

1. Exit Stage Left
2. The Westerlea House Mystery
3. Death Under the Sun
4. The Thirteenth Room
5. The Wrong Man

All titles are available to order from all good book shops.

Signed and personalised books available at adamcroft.net/shop

EBOOK-ONLY SHORT STORIES

- Gone
- The Harder They Fall
- Love You To Death
- The Defender

To find out more, visit adamcroft.net

GET MORE OF MY BOOKS FREE!

Thank you for reading *In Plain Sight*. I hope it was as much fun for you as it was for me writing it.

To say thank you, I'd like to give you some of my books and short stories for FREE. Read on to get yours...

If you enjoyed the book, please do leave a review online. Reviews mean an awful lot to writers and they help us to find new readers more than almost anything else. It would be very much appreciated.

I love hearing from my readers, too, so please do feel free to get in touch with me. You can contact me via my website, on Twitter @adamcroft and you can join my Facebook Readers Group at http://www.facebook.com/groups/adamcroft.

Last of all, but certainly not least, I'd like to let you know that members of my email club have access to FREE, exclusive books and short

stories which aren't available anywhere else. There's a whole lot more, too, so please join the club (for free!) at https://www.adamcroft.net/vip-club

For more information, visit my website: adamcroft.net

Knight & Culverhouse return in

SNAKES & LADDERS

OUT NOW

A trail of death. A web of corruption. The ultimate betrayal.

A series of armed robberies on local petrol stations leaves Mildenheath CID chasing their tails. But things are about to get a whole lot worse.

When an elderly woman is killed during an armed raid on her jewellery shop, Knight and Culverhouse realise one of their own is involved — a police officer.

With the future of Mildenheath CID at stake and the lives of their loved ones under threat, time is running out — fast.

As they begin to investigate the web of corruption, they discover just how deep it runs — and how close to home. But are they prepared for the truth?

Turn the page to read the first chapter...

SNAKES & LADDERS
CHAPTER 1

For Maisie Daniels, there was nothing quite like the hit of cold, fresh morning air on the lungs. It always gave her a real high, and she loved the feel of her body aching as she pushed through the last couple of kilometres of her run.

It was running that'd made her realise she'd needed to leave Milo a few months earlier. She sometimes chuckled at the comparison, enjoying that early morning rush on her lungs and being left with an aching body. Then again, running was a lot healthier than smoking drugs and Milo kicking seven shades of shit out of her.

She'd seen so many people doing the 'new me' thing on Instagram, sharing their exercise routines, fun days out and pert little bodies after a particularly nasty break-up, and it was all so shallow and transparent. If their lives were so great and fulfilled, why did they feel the need to make such a point of it? Maisie half-remembered a quote from some-where or other. *The lady doth protest too much.* No, she'd take much more pleasure from quietly and surreptitiously improving her life until that inevitable day when she'd pass Milo or one of his friends — and there weren't many — in the street. That would be so, so much sweeter. She knew that day could come at any time. It could be tomorrow, it could be today. And that pushed her on at every moment, made her work harder, run faster and push through that wall to get as fit as she possibly could.

She glanced at her watch to check her heart rate as she ran down Naismith Road, towards Mildenheath Woods. Not bad, but she could do with picking up the pace before she got onto uneven ground.

She pushed on further, feeling the burn in her legs and the cold air in her lungs, thinking only of that moment when she finally bumped into Milo and saw his face and how gutted he felt at having chosen a drug over her — the opposite choice to the one she'd made.

Before long, she was turning off the pavement and into Mildenheath Woods, the morning sun breaking through the clouds, beginning to take the chill off the edge of the air. After a minute or so, Maisie realised she'd been pushing it too far. The burn in her lungs was too intense, so she slowed down to a walk while she regained her breath.

Feeling her breathing starting to ease a little, she picked up the pace and walked further along the trail, feeling as though she might be ready to break into a jog again soon. Before she could, her eyes were drawn to a mound of disturbed earth, a few feet off the side of the trail. It seemed incongruous, the leaves having clearly been moved very recently. It didn't look like it'd been done by a fox or a badger, either; it was all too neat, too large.

She felt her heart skip a beat as the potential significance dawned on her. *Don't be silly, Maisie*, she told herself. Two years with Milo had made her automatically assume the worst in any situation. This didn't necessarily mean...

She had to find out. She pulled a chunk of bark loose from a nearby tree and started to dig, raking the loose, rich soil away. But as she removed the top layer of soil and revealed what was beneath, she quickly wished she hadn't.

SNAKES & LADDERS
OUT NOW